Praise for *Two Roads Diverged* and
Melanie Mayer Consulting

"I just wanted to say that the workshop I took with you at Region 20 in July was by far the best one I've been to. I used your technique with my dual credit kids on their first essay, and it was amazing at how it changed things for them! I am taking forever to read [your book], because I truly am looking at things differently."

—Courtney Davila Gonzalez, teacher

"Your training (and these [Facebook] posts) was the most practical and useful one I have ever been to. Thank you for changing my life as a teacher!"

—Kim Fabean, teacher

"I found [*Two Roads Diverged*] thought provoking, practical, and engaging, at a time when I'm evaluating the holes in both my own education and that of my children. The author makes a strong argument for noticing and appreciating the art of language in teaching writing. She then backs up her idea, with research and pragmatic tools, that this task can and must be done, even in an age of testing."

—Susan Crockett, review on *Amazon*

MILES TO GO

Also by Melanie Mayer

Two Roads Diverged and I Took Both:
Meaningful Writing Instruction
in an Age of Testing

MILES
TO GO

WHAT I LEARNED
WHILE I WAS
TEACHING

MELANIE MAYER

TATE PUBLISHING
AND ENTERPRISES, LLC

Published by Tate Publishing & Enterprises, LLC
127 E. Trade Center Terrace | Mustang, Oklahoma 73064 USA
1.888.361.9473 | www.tatepublishing.com

Tate Publishing is committed to excellence in the publishing industry. The company reflects the philosophy established by the founders, based on Psalm 68:11,
"The Lord gave the word and great was the company of those who published it."

Book design copyright © 2015 by Tate Publishing, LLC. All rights reserved.
Cover design by Ivan Charlem Igot
Interior design by Honeylette Pino

Published in the United States of America

ISBN: 978-1-68028-678-6
1. Education / Language / Arts
2. Education / General
15.02.25

This book is dedicated in loving memory to my parents,
Wally and Jean Mayer,
who together are what I have always wanted to be.
I miss you tomorrow.

ACKNOWLEDGMENTS

I have attended numerous sessions and trainings and read countless articles over the course of my career. If, when reading this book, you see something that is eerily familiar—perhaps even something you are already doing in your own classroom—it may be that I, too, first heard it elsewhere. But this is crucial to any group of professionals with such a noble aim as ours: we must help each other. Thank you to all who have helped me. Any imitation is intended as the sincerest form of flattery, not thievery.

Thank you to my colleagues, past and present, at the Port Aransas Independent School District in Port Aransas, Texas. You have made me better.

To Tiara Followell: Why use euphemistic rhetoric? You rock. You have taught me that friendship is a verb, and glitter is a color; and you daily flood my life with both.

To my students: You have been a source of great joy to me. I hope you learned half as much from me as I did from you. And to their parents: Thank you for trusting me.

Finally, I would like to thank my family: My beloved and precious parents, to whom this book is dedicated; my brother, Randy, probably the smartest and hardest working man I know, and one of the best educators to ever serve; my dear sister-in-law, LeeEllen (thank God for your grace, your heart), who is also a great educator; my beautiful, brave, fun sister, Shelley, the Tigger to my Eeyore, Lucy to my Chuck; my dearest friend, Toppy, also a retired teacher, whose constant efforts to keep me from over-scheduling myself (too much spaghetti!) repeatedly fail. And thank you to my nieces and nephews: Kaitlin, Garrett, Jackson, Gage, Weston, Kamryn, and Lincoln, because I love being your "Omie."

I carry your heart.

Thanks also to my Almighty God who has His hand on me always. I am ever thankful, ever mindful of the responsibility that comes with such great blessings.

Contents

Foreword.. 13

Chapter One: Introduction
A New Fantastic Point Of View.............................. 17

Chapter Two
Why—And How—
We Must Still Teach Literature 35

Chapter Three
Reading Non-Fiction And Informational Texts 69

Chapter Four
How To Really Teach Writing................................. 103

Chapter Five
A Place For Grace 133

Chapter Six
Feedback & Grading 153
Chapter Seven
The Power Of Reflection 175
Chapter Eight: Conclusion
Miles To Go 195
Afterword
From Melanie Mayer Consulting 203
Sources 245
Notes And Reflection 249

FOREWORD

By Tiara Followell

If you've had the pleasure of seeing Melanie Mayer in action or of reading her first book, *Two Roads Diverged and I Took Both*, then you have undoubtedly asked yourself: *Is she really that good?*

The answer is yes.

I can say this in complete honesty. I was her student a few years back (okay, 15, but who's counting, really?) and I am now her colleague, a relationship crucial to the majority of the success I have experienced professionally. And through this, I have come to consider her one of my dearest friends. She has and continues to anchor me in growth and love.

As I read her students' passages in this and her previous book, I'm reminded of her influence in my life and learning when I was young. I actually still have an essay I wrote during my freshman year in college about her. It reflects the same theme she discusses in her first chapter: she "opened up a space in my mind that I'd never known needed light." I remember her class vividly. It was when I fell in love with reading. More importantly, it was the first time I felt validated as a writer. This validation meant everything. But we will get back to that.

Fast forward to the present. Melanie and I now teach next door to one another. Things have changed, and yet she continues to flood my life with light. I am constantly in awe of what I witness from her. Everything you read in her books is honestly and constantly what occurs in her classroom. She is that good. Actually, she's better; she's just too humble to realize it.

In these pages, you will read of a teacher's struggles as well as her successes. She will provide strategies for overcoming the first to experience more of the second. You will have moments of: *Why didn't I think of that?* You will also certainly see what makes Melanie Mayer an expert in the art and science of teaching. If you struggle in your classroom, if you find yourself feeling defeated, this book will help you. It will remind you of why you do what you do.

Now, if you want to be a better teacher, if you genuinely love your students and want nothing more than to positively impact not just their education, but their lives, you *must* read this book. In it Melanie shares with you what she shared with me so long ago—the power of validation. She understands that focusing on a *subject* while ignoring the *student* is completely counterproductive. If students don't see themselves as capable and worthy of greatness and success, nothing you do—no amount of content knowledge or passion—will matter.

That is the real magic of this book. It imparts the knowledge of how to truly reach students through effective, meaningful teaching. This book is full of light.

CHAPTER ONE: INTRODUCTION

A NEW FANTASTIC POINT OF VIEW

"I can open your eyes/Take you wonder by wonder…
A whole new world/ A new fantastic point of view"

—Aladdin: A Whole New World Lyrics

INTRODUCTION

A NEW FANTASTIC POINT OF VIEW

"I had never seen a black Jesus before, and this sight both knocked me for a loop and opened up a space in my mind that I'd never known needed light." So says the twelve year old white narrator in Robert McCammon's *A Boy's Life*, upon entering a black person's home for the first time, and seeing a portrait hanging on the wall of a black Jesus wearing a crown of thorns. This is one of the most beautiful, most insightful, and true sentences I have ever read. It lingered on my mind long after I read the book, an expression of the often unwitting, but not malicious, ignorance that plagues humanity. At some point, though, I also realized that what happened to that twelve-year old has also happened to me in the last ten years of my teaching career. Spaces are constantly being opened, by students, or workshops, or colleagues, or books, or articles in journals—*spaces that I'd never known needed light.*

I am overwhelmed and a little embarrassed by the sheer number of new things I have learned in the last few years of my career that I never even knew I needed to learn. Again and again in my classroom, I have put to the test new research-based instructional strategies, ideas for classroom management, and theories on teaching reading and writing, resulting in increased student engagement and achievement. Simple instructional adjustments, such as practices of providing feedback and allowing time for reflection, a shift to more skills-based instruction, and a renewed belief in relationships and the amazing power of grace, have transformed my thinking and my classroom. I am excited that I, the "master" teacher, am learning so much so fast about my profession and myself now, as I approach my twenty-eighth year in the classroom. I am so grateful for these lights shining into "spaces that I'd never known needed light," allowing me to consider that my ways aren't the best or only ways to teach.

Mahatma Gandhi said, "Be the change you wish to see." For a long time, that was easy for me. I wished to see none. As I have matured, I realize my personality type, my very nature, is to resist change. I have threadbare jeans. I have had the same haircut for two decades. I drive the same car until it won't run. Rearranging the furniture just doesn't occur to me. This contentment with status quo has seeped into my professional life over the years as well. Not surprisingly a confirmed Luddite, I was the last one on our campus to get email. Frankly, I didn't see the point. We are a small district. If they needed me, my colleagues could just yell down the hall, or walk the one hundred meters to my classroom and poke their heads in the door.

By the time I got an active email account and realized I could not live without it, my students informed me that email "was so five years ago." This is akin to finally learning (sort of) to use a digital camera, only to have a young friend scoff, "You carry a camera *and* a phone?" I am currently hoping no one notices that I don't tweet so I can skip straight to whatever comes next.

My point is this: I do not enjoy change. I was convinced no one would ever again learn in my classroom when my chalkboard was replaced with a white board, much in the same way I didn't see the point in using a visual presenter named after a *Sesame Street* character (ELMO) or giving students iPads for instruction. My students have always known I care about them. While in my classroom, they learn to read well and write correctly and effectively, and they emerge ready for college. Compared to their peers around the country, I believed my students were heads above the field. Consequently, "If it ain't broke, don't fix it" was a motto I embraced for years.

I wasn't rude, or a rebel. Mine wasn't an outward refusal to change. It was more of a passive-aggressive resistance, the kind where I smile and nod in affirmation at the latest in a long line of new-fangled ideas, fads, trends, proposals, or paradigms in education (even the word "paradigm" was a fad—remember?) and then quietly do everything the way I always have. I was a good teacher; some would say a very good teacher. But while as an individual I had always been committed to personal growth, lifelong learning, and to being the best I could be in various areas of spiritual, intellectual, and physical health, I had not connected this philosophy or mindset to my role as an educator. I had no idea that as a classroom teacher, even a successful one, I had basically "capped" my growth by resting in my own complacency. John Maxwell explains it like this:

> One of the dangers of success is that it can make a person un-teachable. Many people are tempted to use their success as permission to discontinue their growth. They become convinced that they know enough to succeed and they begin to coast. They trade innovation and growth for a formula, which they follow time after time. 'You can't argue with success,' they say. But they're wrong. Why? Because the skills that got you here are probably not the skills that will get you there. (Maxwell, 2012).

One day I realized there was a question bouncing around the recesses of my mind: Is it worth it at this stage of my career to go to workshops, read articles on education, learn the new technology, and possibly change my methods, materials, or syllabi, to perhaps better engage and empower today's students for their lives and careers outside and beyond my classroom? Or could I coast?

I remember the exact moment I realized I wanted to do more than coast. I was teaching a class and suddenly realized I was bored. Not just distracted. Bored. I found myself making my grocery list at the podium while a student read aloud from the book. And I realized if I was bored in my own class, how boring it must be to my students! It struck me then how far I was from that *Promised Land* I had envisioned for my classroom when I became a teacher. I had such dreams of my students reading everything I assigned, having insightful conversations about literature, and sharing writing that moved us all to tears. Mine would be the class students were eager to attend, and for which everyone was always prepared! I wanted this *Promised Land* to exist, but as the years went by, I was like the Israelites in the desert, walking around the same mountain, again and again, year after year, doing the same thing, in the same ways, and with the same results. What should have been an eleven-day trip, at this rate, really was going to take forty years. My students' essays all sounded and looked the same;

they insisted poetry was for barefoot beatniks and *because* was a verb; and I was making grocery lists during class.

This was a most distressing wake-up call for me. I did not want to be boring, or to waste my students' time, because one of my own pet peeves is having my own time wasted. As a Christian, I also believe I serve the Lord through my work, so offering anything less than my best is not appropriate service to Him. Plus, I love reading, and writing, and I believe these skills change and enrich lives and open doors. I knew I had some decisions to make.

I began to reflect and really question myself: What is my philosophy? Why do I teach? What do my students really need to learn? After all, I became a teacher to teach *people,* not teach content; to empower students to live the lives they could only imagine, not to live *my* life; and even more so, to prepare them for possibilities they can't presently imagine or foresee. I became a teacher not so *I* could sit around reading and writing great literature for *my* own purposes—but so that I could teach my students to read and write *for theirs.* Life is fluid. Education is evolving. Literacy is a moving target. Holy cow, I realized, there is no time to coast! Just the opposite! From that point on, I determined to once again passionately pursue best practices for teaching and living. I would examine every choice, plan engaging instruction, and radiate as much excitement on the outside with my students and colleagues about teaching, and education, that I still felt on the inside. I determined to make a difference not only for my own students, but also for my profession.

This did not mean I had to rush out and change everything. It meant simply that I had to *evaluate* everything. If the lesson was boring or habitual, and did not involve a specific skill my students could use, it had to be changed or eliminated. If the lesson was in an area in which I had a lot of knowledge (or *files*), or was something I enjoyed but which could not really be defended, it had to go. Part of intentional instructional planning, I have learned, is considering what to hold, and what to let go. I had to change, but only when to do so would enhance student learning.

One of the pitfalls in education, perhaps in any field, is to "throw the baby out with the bathwater," if you'll pardon the cliché. We change *too much*; we swing like a pendulum from one side of the spectrum or philosophy to the other as political, economic, or social climate dictates. We have done this with grammar instruction, reading instruction, and inclusion, just to name a few. We are in danger of doing this with new technology now. Using technology in the classroom to do the same things we can do without it, just to say we are using it, is not necessarily positive change. And allowing students to let the technology do their thinking for them would actually be a giant step backward. Change for the sake of change is not the goal; but for me, change had to become at least a real option.

I have learned that most content can be changed, but most values and skills must be retained. I must consider what is essential for my students to know and be able to do, and what is non-essential, flexible, arbitrary, or fluff. I do not think my students will remember all the things Queen Elizabeth did for England during the Renaissance, or the names of the rulers of the Tudor Dynasty, or even what happens, in order, in each of Shakespeare's tragedies. These are not values. But to be able to read Shakespeare's writing and understand it is to realize that the language is "magical," as one student reflected. This is a valuable skill. The power of language will resonate in their favorite lines from his plays and sonnets, and they will "feel smarter for knowing them," as another student proclaimed.

Indeed,

> We know why the opening lines of Romeo and Juliet, 'Two households, both alike in dignity/In fair Verona where we lay our scene,' sound infinitely better than the Shakespeare Made Easy version, 'The play is set in beautiful Verona in Italy.' Or why Shakespeare's 'From forth the fatal loins of these two foes/A pair of star-crossed lovers take their life' sounds better than the No Fear version, 'Two unlucky children of these enemy families become lovers and commit suicide.' (LoMonico, 2012)

When we summarize reading for our students, or give them abridged or modern versions, we are implying that *what happened* is all that is important. But that just isn't true. The reading itself is important. We must teach our students that when reading Shakespeare, the magic carpet ride *is* the destination. This is a value we must keep. W.H. Auden said, "We would rather be ruined than changed." At the same time, there are things that change may ruin. For me, the point was simply to begin to consider if, when, and where changes were warranted, in an effort to give my students the best preparation- and best education- possible.

There's a certain store I call the devil store. I enter it not knowing I need anything. Upon walking the aisles, however, I am immediately struck by the number of delightful gadgets and items without which I cannot live. This often expensive realization is not unlike what we desire for our students: Here is some poetry. Wow! I need that. And here: persuasive writing. I can use that! And here, a character like me; I must know what decisions he makes and how it will end. Reading and writing are cognitive skills that must be taught. The abilities to decipher text and to articulate meaning are values that must be retained. I have learned, though, that the packaging, advertising, delivery, and even the product and assessment of learning, can and should be changed. Those exact same items, when they are not in the devil store, do not appeal to me near as much. Our students are consumers in a fast-paced, technologically stimulating world. We must present our subject matter and skills to students in such a way that they are shocked and surprised to find these are things they have needed all along to enrich the spaces of their lives.

Writing has evolved. The five paragraph essay, while still a solid organization method, has transitioned into online writing, which includes shorter, more frequent paragraphs, links to research and photos and websites, and text boxes with word counts. Students use more and more text with bulleted lists, hyperlinks, headings and subheadings, and shorter paragraphs. These things are reader-friendly. "In a world where humans are becoming overwhelmed by volume, do students still need to practice composing long essays— or should they learn to powerfully condense their thoughts into pithy paragraphs and tweets? Far too many people still wrongly associate length with depth." (Prensky, 2013). The values we must keep are the depth and organization—and Standard Academic English (SAE). It is *not* okay for our students to write for academic purposes and audiences the way they do on social media.

But it *is* acceptable to redesign our products. If I am giving the same assignments, with the same rubrics, as I was twenty years ago, I am doing my students a disservice. They must learn from me how to write for *their* purposes and times and audiences, in various and current forms and styles.

I like reading and writing. Most of my students, however, don't like reading, and they especially do not like to read the things I like to read, which more often than not are the things teachers assign. They do not like to write, in part because they do not know *how* to write. I have learned that teaching is hard work. Whether or not a student has a natural affinity or ability for any subject, learning doesn't just happen. We have to cause it. We have to work at making it happen. Teaching is not about hope. It's about purposeful instructional planning (with students' individual learning profiles in mind) that aims at ensuring high-level success for each student (Tomlinson and Javius, 2012). I can't take for granted that if I provide a writing environment, and give my students adequate inspiration and motivation, meaningful topics, and even an audience they care about—all the things various speakers, educators, authors, and presenters have advocated at one time or another— they will produce quality writing. *We still have to teach them how to write.*

Peg Tyre, author of *The Trouble With Boys: A Surprising Report Card on Our Sons*, said in her address to the Conference on English Leadership (November, 2012) that boys often fall behind in writing because they especially need explicit instruction, not just a "writing environment." They need to have a plan and some tools, which allow them to feel in control. Tyre points out that when teachers say "we teach writing," unfortunately what we often mean instead is "we teach writing to kids we can teach"—not to everybody. We need to teach our lowest performing students to write. And this requires explicit, building block instruction. What constitutes good writing? What goes first? How do you get from point A to point B? What words indicate an example is coming? What is evidence and how do you cite it? How do you punctuate a list? A title? A possessive noun? How do you use a semi-colon? When are fragments effective? We must not take these things for granted, or be reluctant to spend time in the trenches practicing them.

What if, when learning to drive, I was given keys, a nice car, an important place to get to that I really wanted to go, and even told how to start the car? I need to know more than that, don't I? What are the rules? How do I parallel park? Why must I signal? How do I turn? How do I brake? How do I drive on ice? Where are the lights? What if it rains? What if I need to drive in New York? Atlanta? God forbid, England? Yikes! The same concept is true for reading, and writing.

Some of what I have learned while teaching has been content-related. I gain new insight every time I reread certain poems, plays, or novels. I learn a little bit more about authors, literature, various genres, and writing each year. More of what I have learned has been about delivering engaging instruction for all students, regardless of their personal situation, background, ability level, or opportunities outside of school. I have learned that feedback is a more effective teaching tool than lecture, and that it is only during reflection that we—both students and teachers—realize what we have learned and how to apply it to our lives.

But most of what I have learned while teaching is linked to areas of personal growth. I have learned that it's not about me. It doesn't matter what I enjoy, am good at, or know; what counts at the end of the day is *what my students learn, and can do.* I have learned there are many ways to teach and to learn. I have learned that grading is not a black and white—or red—issue; that grace has the power to save more minds than justice; that positive change won't kill me and in fact may be beneficial; and that growth happens throughout life if we are just willing to open up our minds and let the light shine in, even if we think we can see just fine.

There is a story about a farmer who was looking for a hired hand. Desperate, he advertised for help, and for a long time, no one came. Then a raggedy old man staggered up the walk and announced he would like to work. The farmer asked him for a resume; he produced instead a crumpled piece of paper from a pocket with the words: "He sleeps in the storm." The farmer did not know what this could mean, and tossed it aside, but hired the old man, because he really needed some help on the farm. A few weeks went by, and an awful storm came. Thunder roared, lightning flashed, rain poured down, and the wind blew the trees sideways. The farmer woke up, terrified, and screamed for his hired hand. He didn't answer.

The farmer ran out to the barn, expecting the worse. But the animals were in their stalls, with feed, and the barn was secure. He ran to the pasture, and found the hay baled, bound, and covered in tarps. He ran to the hired hand's quarters and burst through the doors—and the old man was sound asleep. It was then that the farmer remembered the piece of paper: "He sleeps in the storm." And he got it. He realized the old man could sleep in the storm, because he had already done everything he was supposed to do, the best he could, before the storm came.

I believe we can apply this to teaching. If we as teachers take responsibility to stay abreast of the research and the latest opportunities and possibilities for instruction in our field; if every day, week, and year we do what we know is right and best for our students; then when the storms come, whether in the form of budget cuts, new standards, new technology, new assessments, or something else, we can rest easy. We can sleep in the storm.

Teaching is a science *and* an art, which requires constant renewing of both the mind and the heart. These are the concepts and instructional strategies that work for me in my classroom. I wish there was a way I could have known it all when I first began. But like reading the works of great writers, teaching is something of a magic carpet ride in itself. Knowledge can be sought, and discovered, but true wisdom and understanding are gained only in the evaluated experience. Still, wishing I had had a book about all this all along prompts me to write this one. I hope it is helpful and encouraging to teachers out there, or at least, makes you smile.

Blessings,
Melanie

Notes and Reflection

CHAPTER TWO

WHY—AND HOW— WE MUST STILL TEACH LITERATURE

"Books are a uniquely portable magic."

—Stephen King, *On Writing*

CHAPTER 2

WHY—AND HOW—
WE MUST STILL TEACH
LITERATURE

In "Your Brain on Fiction," Anne Murphy Paul cites research proving that reading narratives activates many other parts of our brains; that stories mirror real life and so does our brain activity while reading them. It appears that reading is good for you. This reminds me of a few years ago when scientists reported on a popular TV news program that there was startling new evidence that "prayer works!" Even though I already knew that, I suppose it is nice to be affirmed. Literature is an important part of the ELA classroom, but only if students are taught to read it and inspired to embrace it.

Fiction has always comprised the majority of reading instruction and experiences of students in schools. However, in recent decades, our students have learned to read this fiction specifically to recall basic information, detail, and literary elements such as plot outline, setting, or theme—not really to engage with and experience the whole text. They can recall the order of events, but can't tell you why the characters behaved the way they did. They can recite the main idea, but can't articulate how the writer's approach to the topic facilitated their understanding. Our students can scan a text for the setting, but can rarely recall a book or story that has changed their thinking about something forever.

For years, I assumed too much: I assumed my secondary students were not reading because they were lazy, or just hadn't found the right book yet. I assumed they would read the full-length novels I assigned if I "hooked" them with exciting and suspenseful book talks, and held them accountable with periodic reading quizzes; then, after they read, they would "get it," and they, too, would find themselves holding the book to their chests, unable to move or breathe, so touched by the writer's words. But inevitably, year after year I found myself assigning failing grades on reading quizzes, or reading answers taken directly from "Spark Notes," and having discussions about the book with myself.

As many other English teachers experienced this more and more, a movement to quit teaching full-length texts altogether began to gather steam. I have learned, though, that reading literature is a value that must be retained; and there are many things our secondary students don't know, like why they need it and how to read it, that we can and should teach them.

The first challenge is to instill the value of the reading experience itself: the why. Students today are not sure of the need for or relevance of traditional print full length novels.

> As English teachers, our role is to change students' perceptions about the value of literature. We want them to love literature as much as we do. We won't do that by just getting our students to create vocabulary lists from *The Scarlet Letter*, or to identify the major characters in *Lord of the Flies* and create a Venn diagram with them, or to keep a journal listing the major themes of *The Great Gatsby*, or answer lots of plot-related questions about *Macbeth*. If that were enough, we could skip reading completely (something many students already do) and just pass out plot summaries, character sketches, and lists of themes. (LoMonico, 2012)

We who have experienced the appreciation and catharsis that reading provides, know reading is a journey we take with the writer, not a treasure hunt for the main ideas (Newkirk, 2012). We have to make reading not solely about what happened, but a worthy experience in and of itself. Reading the actual book versus reading the online notes is akin to participating in anything from river rafting to sex: Would you rather experience it for yourself or have someone just tell you about it? Knowing what happens in a book is not the same as *experiencing* the book, just as knowing how skydiving works is hardly the same as doing it yourself.

Too often students are allowed to slide by, to get away with *not reading* by participating in discussions in which the teacher, or another student, basically tells them what happened in the book. "If we use study guides, comprehension quizzes, pseudo whole-class 'discussions,' that serve mainly to summarize and interpret the reading…we send the message to students that no engaged reading or individual interpretation of the text is necessary and that *not reading* the text is just fine." (Broz, 2011) Spark notes, teacher summaries, abridged versions, and study guides often send the message that the content is more important than our interaction with it or the personal experiences we bring to it and take from it. But reading literature is not just about the content. So first, we must endeavor to have students understand and crave the benefits of reading literature themselves.

The greatest benefits and lessons of literature are often affective. The reading of carefully selected literature can teach students empathy, tolerance, civility, open-mindedness, self-awareness, and compassion. James Baldwin said, "You think your pain and your heartbreak are unprecedented in the history of the world, but then you read. It was books that taught me that the things that tormented me most were the very things that connected me with all the people who were alive, or who had ever been alive." Indeed, as over time I have experienced more of life's grief and joy, I find myself suddenly understanding some parts of the literature I have read for years. My experiences outside of the text have altered my experiences with the text. Likewise, reading provides insight, preparation, and compassion for events and people we may encounter in the future.

In their article, "Literature as a 21st Century Skill," Kylene Beers and Robert E. Probst advocate teaching and reading literature for its ability to humanize us, and echo that simply reading for information cheats students out of that benefit:

> How is it that students who read about human endeavor and suffering can be casually, callously indifferent to the struggles and pains of the kids who sit at the desks next to them...Is it because Narnia isn't a land where you discover your own courage but is a place to discuss how setting affects the plot? Perhaps it is because the bridge to Terabithia has become a true/false question about sequencing: Jessie lost the race to Leslie *before* they crossed the bridge to Terabithia. (Beers & Probst, 2011)

Even though I agreed philosophically with Beers and Probst, with LoMonico, Newkirk, Broz, and a host of others who advocate reading literature holistically and humanely; and even though I am an avid reader and lover of literature myself; for years my classroom practices did not reflect this.

I practiced all the things that the experts say make kids skip or hate reading, and miss the purpose and pleasure of it altogether. I gave quizzes to hold them accountable, thinking that would force them to read. I talked about what happened in the books, assuming they needed to know all these great stories. But I finally realized that students (indeed, all readers) care far more about the implication of what happens in a text than the facts themselves; the connections they make (which are not all the same); and the way the writer makes them feel. Only recently have I come to understand that just knowing what happens in any book is useless knowledge. The affective value of reading is different for all of us; it is an experience we share with the writer.

Just last week I cared so much about characters in a book I was reading I thought about them before I went to sleep. I hurt with them. I loved with them. I wondered what might have been different. No one can make you feel that by summarizing a story. The point is to read the book and make your own meaning. Our students need to see themselves in characters they read. They need to know they are not alone; that the world they live in is not the entire world that is; and that there is something to be gained from shared human experiences. This is a great benefit of reading literature, and why it must never be removed from an educational curriculum that includes "humanities." When I started emphasizing the affective side of reading, more of my students were motivated to actually read the books.

We can't expect, however, that students will read as many full-length texts in the course of a school year as we used to assign. Personal, online, or digital reading outside the school setting, the increased reading load in other classes, and our own curriculum requirements have changed. In order to address the need for informational and non-fiction reading material, and current and new literacies, I often use excerpts from full-length novels to instruct students in style, voice, or various literary or rhetorical techniques. But there is still a place for reading entire works of literature, with benefits beyond what assessments measure.

Since we can't read everything with our students that we would like to, it becomes imperative that we choose the full-length texts we assign carefully. We must realize that for most students who enter our classrooms today, reading is not a hobby, but a chore. We can't expect today's students to read what we were assigned in school, or even what we used to assign just two decades ago. Likewise, we can't expect them to all enjoy the same books we do. Recently I was asked what novels I require my senior high school students to read. My answer is that it depends on my students. The same novels won't work for every class, every year. We must consider that we are helping to define a child's literacy experience, and what he or she will forever associate with reading. To ensure that more of our students will read, we must choose literature wisely.

First, get student input on reading selections. Remember, most content can be changed; the reading itself is the value we want to retain. Give them a choice of two or three full-length books to read as a class. Perhaps allow all students to read the first chapter and one other of two different books, discuss them as a class, and decide together, or vote. This creates buy-in, in addition to helping you choose books for students that they will actually enjoy. One year my class wants to read *Frankenstein* (Shelly); one year, *Pride and Prejudice* (Austen); another, *The Life of Pi* (Martel). They want to read *The Secret Life of Bees* (Kidd) instead of *The Adventures of Huckleberry Finn* (Twain) most years. One class was so evenly divided between *Peace Like a River* (Enger) and *The Poisonwood Bible (Kingsolver)*, we just did both simultaneously; I allowed each group of students to read their choice. A bonus to this was that their enthusiasm about their respective books was catching, and many students ended up reading both novels. Sometimes I know what book will entertain a certain group of students, but other times, I totally miss the mark. I have abandoned a book mid-stream because I realized no one was reading. Remember, while perseverance is indeed a valued skill, our responsibility is to teach *reading*.

Students may keep and use a reader's notebook for a variety of purposes. They could make connections to today's world; make inferences, with text evidence for support; and list questions they have about events in the novel and writer choices. They could choose favorite quotes to read aloud to the class, with explanation of why they are their favorites. They should list page numbers for all of this so they can easily direct their reading group or the class to the section for discussion.

It is a reality that all students use online novel notes. This is nothing new; just the other day I mentioned a novel my students were reading and my brother asked, "Was that a thin yellow and black paperback? I read that!" (He was referring to Cliff Notes. Remember those?) We had to go buy those at a bookstore; students today have access to much more than this at the click of a mouse. Instead of fighting this, I first try to make the reading experience appealing and interactive enough that they want to read the full text, and need to in order to participate in all of our activities and discussions. Also, I use these online notes too, and have students bring to the discussion (in their readers' notebooks) things that are *not* in these online notes, but that they felt were significant to the experience of reading the text.

Pick and choose; you won't want to have students do all of these activities for every section, chapter, or novel that they read. The last thing we want to do is make the reading experience tedious or choppy because students constantly must stop reading to write in a notebook. We have to find the right balance between engagement and accountability, which should be supporting and not opposing goals.

There is a cognitive side to reading both literature and informational texts, which actually helps students to fully realize the affective value. This is when we read to understand the writer's craft—not just the plot, or the characters, or the setting, or figurative language—but the *why* and the *how* behind them, the way the author manipulates readers to achieve his purpose, whether intrigue, emotion, awareness, or passion.

> What's wrong with teaching plot, character, and theme? Nothing, really, as long as teachers work with students to look closely at the text and the writer's style and word choice…What worries me is that sometimes, in teaching all the elements of a literary work and the author's life, we end up teaching about the novel instead of teaching the novel itself. (LoMonico, 2012)

There are specific things we can teach about the craft of writing that provide motivation and access to texts, and result in richer, more meaningful reading experiences for students.

Increasing students' background knowledge is a first step in enhancing their ability to not only read but also enjoy literature, including full-length novels, short stories, and poetry. I use *How to Read Literature Like a Professor* (Foster, 2003), and *Reading Like a Writer* (Prose, 2007) as texts in my classroom to empower students early in our literature studies. For the rest of the year, they know: If he takes a trip, it is probably a quest, and this means he will learn something about himself and be changed. If it rains on her, or she falls in a river, and doesn't drown, consider whether she comes away "reborn," or changed; it may be a symbolic baptism.

Foster's book introduces students to what setting and symbols could mean, and why authors may include dialogue, violence, or even sex. Prose shows them how close reading can make them better writers. These texts make them aware that everything is significant. From colors and rain to sentence structure and punctuation, there are no accidents. Their background knowledge and ability to read literature increase exponentially from reading these texts. And, they absolutely love knowing these things! They feel suddenly privy to all these secrets about literature, and they look for them in everything we read. I have to remind them that their newfound knowledge must be substantiated by text evidence, however, as they tend to make random objects phallic symbols, or stepping into a puddle a baptism.

A brief study of psychology gives students insight into character motivation. For example, we talk about Freud's theory of the human mind (id, ego, and super-ego), Jung's theory of individuation (shadow, persona, and anima), defense mechanisms (rationalization, repression, projection, regression, sublimation, and reaction formation), archetypes (colors, numbers, the Garden, the Serpent, the hero, and Death), and more, to examine *why* characters do the things they do. This type of study brings characters, settings, and events to life for readers and causes real heartfelt interaction with the text. Does Armand project his own self-loathing onto Desiree in Chopin's "Desiree's Baby"? Do the student's repressed sexual desires finally catch up to him in "The Adventures of the German Student"? How do the female characters in *Heart of Darkness* represent the dual nature of Kurtz' personality? With this background knowledge, students feel so much smarter and sophisticated and confident in their approach to literature; our discussions have depth and merit; and their reading experiences are enhanced on an affective level as well.

In addition to increasing students' literary background knowledge so they may recognize the *things* that are significant, we also want to teach them that the *style* is significant. "If we want students to actually read assigned books, we have to go beyond [teaching **about** the novel] and have students look closely at the author's actual words." (Lomonico, 2012) The writer makes very purposeful choices in language as well as in events, objects, and characterization. We have always taught the definitions of literary elements, such as plot outline, setting, allusion, metaphor, symbolism, and theme, and had students identify these in literature. It requires little more than memorization skills for students to match twenty literary elements to their definitions, and recognize these in text.

For years, questions on standardized tests reinforced this method of teaching: "What was the setting?" Answer: Chicago in the 1960's. "What is the metaphor in line 9 of the poem?" Answer: Man is a machine. These questions stress a low level knowledge of terms but not their purpose, application, or effectiveness in specific texts—and the purpose is really what matters. *Why* is the setting significant in *The Secret Life of Bees* or *The Crucible*? *Why* does the author use a metaphor in line nine of the poem, and *what is the effect on the reader*? Instead of, "What is the point of view of the story?" ask students "How would 'The Story of an Hour' or 'A Rose for Emily' or 'The Tell Tale Heart' (or any other story) be different if it were told from a different point of view?" These types of questions represent a much better, more relevant and meaningful way to study literature. Students need to understand how the literary and stylistic choices writers make contribute to the tone, theme, plot and overall experience of reading.

Students can practice applying their newly acquired background knowledge of literature and rhetoric by using sentence stems to analyze short stories. Sentence stems are invaluable in the classroom to help students understand and use the language of literary analysis, to express what they know articulately, and to write critically and correctly about literature. "***The author uses*** a limited omniscient point of view in 'The Story of an Hour' (Chopin) ***to*** give the reader insight into the primary character's thoughts. ***This shows the reader*** that she doesn't die from the shock and joy that her husband is not dead after all, but from shock and grief that her freedom is lost. If we weren't privy to her thoughts, we, like the other characters, would misinterpret her actions." These sentence stems force students to identify not only the stylistic choices the writer makes (the easier task), but their purpose and effectiveness as well (the more difficult task). Students learn that *what* happens in the literature is not nearly as significant as *why* it happens, and how the author makes readers feel about it. This practical knowledge empowers and informs students' reading and their own writing.

Students enjoy sharing their favorite quotes and lines from each chapter of any full length text we read in class. We discuss why they chose each passage, why they felt the way they did at certain points in the novel, and how they as readers were manipulated by the writer. At times, I have them try to mimic some of the stylistic choices of the authors in their own writing. For example, students who noted that Ernest Hemingway uses dialogue to define his characters, and compound sentences with repetition of certain words and diction to describe scenes, would experiment with these same techniques by rewriting their own personal narratives or short stories *in Hemingway's style*. John Steinbeck uses figurative language, parallel structure, and dialect. Students might discuss the effects of each of these stylistic choices, and try to use them in their own descriptions of everyday life, natural disasters, or colorful characters.

On an exam, then, we would not match definitions; we would read something completely new, and I would ask my students about the effects of the writer's choices, perhaps specifically figurative language, grammar, and point of view (or whatever our lesson focus has been). Students would demonstrate critical reading and writing ability as well as knowledge on an application level, which provides relevance, or as one of my students reflected, "We know *why* we need to learn all this stuff, and it makes us feel smart."

On a recent exam I asked my 11th grade students: "How does John Steinbeck's approach to his topic in *The Grapes of Wrath* make it accessible to readers?" We had completed this novel, both in and out of class, and most students were fairly interested and engaged throughout our studies. They complained that because it was a test, they couldn't use their books to cite text evidence as examples like I taught them; but they nonetheless included many references to the novel from memory and their notebooks. Their answers also reflected knowledge of many of the literary and stylistic elements from Foster's *How to Read Literature Like a Professor* and Prose's *Reading Like a Writer,* such as: Tom's journey as a quest; Casy as a scapegoat archetype; the grandparents' heart trouble as parallel to their real broken hearts; water as a symbol; and Steinbeck's repetition and parallelism to emphasize the loss of belongings and dignity.

Here is one student's answer. I wish I could show you her growth from when we first approached a question like this at the beginning of the year.

> In *The Grapes of Wrath*, Steinbeck uses many different ways of making his work more accessible to the reader. One way he accomplishes this is through his use of literary devices. Steinbeck uses many different forms of repetition to get his point across. For example, in the beginning of the novel when describing the land and weather, Steinbeck continually is saying how dry and empty and barren the land is. This repetition makes readers think it has been that way a long time, and is like that as far as you can see. It is miserable. Another literary device he uses is imagery. Steinbeck is very vivid in his writing technique, which helps the reader better comprehend what it was like to live during the dust bowl.
>
> Another example of how Steinbeck's work was accessible to the reader is his use of intercalary chapters throughout the novel. These chapters help readers go from the specific plight of the Joad family to the general situation faced by all, and provide useful background information. Also, they provide mood and themes that were evident throughout the novel. One example of this is the chapter where Steinbeck shows how one of the other Okies' families is low on everything and needs gas and food for their family to survive. This

shows the reader what it was like for everyone all around, and gives a better understanding of the way they all had to pitch in and help. In another one of these chapters a turtle struggles to cross a highway, symbolizing the Joads' journey to California.

And last, Steinbeck helps the reader understand the time and setting of the novel through his use of dialects. This also gives more life and well-roundedness to the characters. For example, the Joads and everyone from the South had very strong accents, and used grammar that related to the time period that *The Grapes of Wrath* was written in. The dialect on the surface though is not as important as the goodness of the characters on the inside.

All of these techniques that Steinbeck used help the reader better understand his novel even though it was a different setting and time period. His writing style provides a more entertaining and enjoyable way for the book to be accessible to readers.

Choosing literature that specific students will enjoy, allowing their input into these choices, and emphasizing the affective benefits of reading are positive steps which will set teachers and students up for success. Increasing their background knowledge and understanding of style will allow students to see the big picture, which further enhances their experience of reading full-length novels. As a bonus, this kind of reading also informs students' own writing. Through full-length literature, we may be transported—and grounded—at once.

Poetry

Just as full-length literature and informational texts are both essential to the development of the whole child or whole ELA classroom, so, too, is poetry. Few things are harder to sell our students on than poetry. I wonder if this is in part because of the poetry to which they are exposed in schools, and the ways in which it is presented.

Consider this example: Mr. Walt Whitman has enjoyed long tenure in the 11th grade ELA textbook. I remember studying his poems when I was a student, and year after year, I had my own students read his poetry in the textbook. In a recent 11th grade class made up of almost all boys, and many of them struggling learners, this was torture. My worst reader and most eager volunteer haltingly spit out the syllables: "I-sound-my-bar-bar-bar-Miss, I don't know this word—("barbaric")-whatever-yelp-("yawp")-whatever-over-the rooftops-of-the-world." I had not pre-taught vocabulary, so my students not only struggled to pronounce the words, but they had no idea what the words meant. They sat there, eyes glazed over, as their classmate mispronounced in monotone the whole of Whitman's poem. Never mind the *Promised Land*; I began praying for the *Rapture*. Suddenly I realized with horror that this was how

I was introducing poetry to my students. This was why they didn't like poetry, and thought it was too hard to understand. It was my fault—and I love poetry!

I went home and contemplated where I had gone so wrong. And I searched for another way to show students the power and beauty of language through poetry. I found a Spoken Word poem on YouTube, called "Knock Knock" by Daniel Beaty. In it he talks about his absent father, whom he had to visit in prison as a young boy, and all the lessons he wished his father could have taught him: "How to shave, how to dribble a ball, how to talk to a lady, how to walk like a man." He proclaims the lesson of his father, and all fathers like him, is not to make the same mistakes, and not to let the fathers' mistakes define the sons. It is a beautiful poem, and he performs it passionately. My students loved it.

They asked me to show them this slam video repeatedly that day. We talked about the very same elements of repetition, catalog, imagery, alliteration, rhyme, rhythm, theme, pacing, and more, that I was hoping to teach through Whitman's poem, "Song of Myself." This was, in fact, a "Song of Myself" that students could understand, and relate to. They discussed why it worked. And one precious lamb asked me at the end of that class period, "Can we do this? Can we have poetry slams, like on Fridays?" I didn't want to seem too eager: "Well, I had planned to teach grammar on Friday, but…I guess we could do that."

My students brought in song lyrics the next three Fridays, read them, and discussed the elements of poetry that contributed to the poignancy and power of each. Then on the fourth Friday, a student read something that his classmates did not recognize. "Dude, where's that from? I don't know that one," one student exclaimed. "I wrote that," the student who had contributed the poem said proudly. "It's mine."

This is not to say there is not a place for the poetry of Walt Whitman in the English classroom today. But literacy evolves. There is now a Levi's commercial which features Whitman's poem, "Pioneers! O Pioneers!" If I were to ask my students to read this poem in a textbook, from the title alone they would surmise that I was a dinosaur. They would think pioneers settled the west two decades ago, and wonder what this poem could possibly offer them today. Hearing it read aloud in the background of this commercial, however, makes Whitman's words come to life for students. They are able to create meaning on many levels, and, subsequently, even enjoy creating their own poetry commercials from classic poetry, using images to convey tone and theme. We must make poetry accessible to our students, in the context of their everyday lives, so they realize that it can be a living, breathing part of *their* literacy experiences, not just something they have to suffer through in English class and forget when they walk out the door.

I used to teach poetry by reading various poems with my students, identifying literary elements therein, and having discussions with myself about why they are beautiful. I'd have students write poetry in sundry patterns, producing a final thematic poetry notebook or project to display on the wall, giving weight to the creativity and neatness of the presentation as well as the writing. Now I try to make poetry part of the whole curriculum and literacy experience, weaving it in with everything we do. I try to present poems from various cultures, in language my students can relate to, with topics and themes they care about.

Recently after reading and writing expository essays, we read "The Problems with Hurricanes," by Victor Hernandez Cruz, and then viewed him reading it to a live audience (YouTube): "With hurricanes it's not the wind, or the noise, or the water…it's the mangoes, avocados, green plantains and bananas flying through town like projectiles." I then had my students write and perform their own informative poems: "The Problems With…" anything they wanted. "The Problems With My English Teacher" was a popular choice, of course. The activity was wildly popular and my students did a great job.

You've heard the expression, "There's an App for that!"? Well, in my classroom, there's a poem for that. Students are encouraged to keep a notebook of their favorite poems or lines throughout the year. The Favorite Poem Project asks ordinary people to recite their favorite poems and talk about why they love them (www.favoritepoem.org—*The Videos*). When I saw this, I realized that very few of my students would be able to name their favorite poems if I asked them; and none would be able to recite one. I consider it a worthy goal to change that. After viewing several of the examples on this website, my students are prompted to be aware throughout the year that they will be required to select and memorize a favorite poem. They may present to the class with a short talk, or film themselves reciting a poem and explaining why they like it, just like the videos on this website. Students may choose from all poems we have read during the year, or from others they discover on their own. Many find that their favorites change throughout the year. There truly is a poem out there that everyone will enjoy.

Bell-ringer exercises can quickly engage students and help them understand the purpose and power of figurative language in poetry and in their own writing. Recently I instructed students: "Write a sentence rich in figurative language that describes how you are feeling today." One student said, "My brain is like a beehive, and my thoughts are bees buzzing and stinging me in all directions."

"Why don't you just say you have a lot on your mind?" I asked. "I wanted to show it was negative, loud, and annoying. You can have a lot on your mind that isn't necessarily bad."

Another wrote that he felt "like a shoelace left untied all day, dragging behind through crap on the floor, stepped on,

tripped over, and not worth the effort to bend over and fix."
I almost sent him to the counselor.

"Why not just say you are sad?" I asked.

"I guess I wanted you to feel sorry for me," he said, "Sad wasn't enough for how I feel today." This short activity helps students tackle changing assessments that require them to move beyond simple recognition into an understanding of the purpose and effects of figurative language.

I also have students read a poem that is rich in figurative language, rewrite it using bland language, and talk about the difference. Consider the following example:

> "The Eagle" by Alfred, Lord Tennyson
>
> He clasps the crag with crooked hands;
> Close to the sun in lonely lands,
> Ring'd with the azure world, he stands.
>
> The wrinkled sea beneath him crawls;
> He watches from his mountain walls,
> And like a thunderbolt he falls.

A bland version might read, "The eagle sits on a mountain next to the sun and looks over the land below, and flies down." Students note the loss of the majestic, arrogant, self-centered point of view and tone that the personification and alliteration in the original poem combine to create. They reflect that no one cares about the eagle in the bland sentence, but in the poem, the eagle is a dynamic force so powerful and confident and "human" it is breath-taking.

Activities such as these increase students' knowledge and appreciation of how and *why* figurative language works, as opposed to just being able to recognize and label various techniques. And students can demonstrate their newfound academic lingo and knowledge about poetry in sentence stems: "**The author uses** the words 'wrinkled' and 'crawls' **to show** how the waves look to the eagle high above. This **personification** emphasizes that it's all about the eagle, from his perspective, and this is how the sea would look to him; it occupies a lowly place in the mind of the eagle."

It is so much more interesting and challenging to ask students *why* the author uses personification, alliteration, or any element of poetic language, instead of just allowing them to identify it. Of course "He **c**lasps the **c**rag with **c**rooked hands" is alliteration. Anyone can plainly see the letter "c" repeated. More worth discussing is *why* it is repeated, and the resulting effect on readers.

Not Your Daughter's Jeans has the right idea. This is not your grandmother's poetry. We may have to change the storefront window to create interest. But once the door to verse is open, readers may well venture down that same hall, and discover the great Romantic poets, poets of the Harlem Renaissance, Frost, Yeats, Neruda, Millay, or Browning. Like reading full-length literature, reading poetry humanizes us. Studying it helps students understand how language works and how writers make effective choices to move readers. Poetry is important just as art and music are important, to the concept of beauty in the world and as part of the education of the whole child. I have learned that poetry is a value that must be retained. How we present it to our students, and which poems we choose for them, are things that can be changed.

No discussion of reading literature in the ELA classroom, even today, would be complete without a nod to William Shakespeare. There is no better teacher than Shakespeare about the magic and power of language, no better place to begin to make reading about language instead of order of events, thematic discussions, philosophical debates, and historical background. I have learned to emphasize this from the beginning of any Shakespeare lesson: what happens in the play is surely important, but not more important than how he relays it to us.

I used to start my "Shakespeare unit" with background notes on the Renaissance: the rulers, inventions, and influences; and background on the Bard's life and legacy. Just as I realized that my passion for reading novels was not evident in my practice of teaching them to students, I have come to understand that the value of Shakespeare is not in the life and times, or even storylines; rather, it is in the words and language, and their effects on readers. I introduce the bard to my students now by reciting excerpts, lines, and phrases. "Tomorrow, and tomorrow, and tomorrow, Creeps in this petty pace from day to day," I sigh, dramatically, as my high school seniors are nearing graduation, and are feeling impatient, and all-too self-important. I continue:

> To the last syllable of recorded time;
> And all our yesterdays have lighted fools
> The way to dusty death. Out, out, brief candle!
> Life's but a walking shadow, a poor player,
> That struts and frets his hour upon the stage,
> And then is heard no more. It is a tale
> Told by an idiot, full of sound and fury,
> Signifying nothing.

What does it mean? Talk, I say. And how do you know what it means? Talk. Why the hyperbole? Why the alliteration? The metaphors? Talk. Write. Use sentence stems. They do. Indeed, how well Shakespeare understood human nature may be second only to how beautifully he expressed human emotion, through purposeful, powerful language techniques.

In fact, I announce, there is probably a line from Shakespeare for every situation they may find themselves in. When facing a tough decision, it is wise to remember the words of Polonius, in Hamlet: "This above all, to thine own self be true,/ and it must follow, as the night the day,/ thou canst not then be false to any man." Ah, interesting. What does it mean? Talk.

I tell students that when opportunity knocks, they must seize it, because:

> There is a tide in the affairs of men.
> Which, taken at the flood, leads on to fortune;
> Omitted, all the voyage of their life
> Is bound in shallows and in miseries.
> On such a full sea are we now afloat,
> And we must take the current when it serves,
> Or lose our ventures.

And I know this, I tell them; I know that there have been such tides in my own life, and some I have taken, and some I have missed. Living in an island town on a beach in the Gulf of Mexico, my students are particularly receptive to this imagery; they can easily imagine the shallows, the full sea, the one chance to catch the tide and ride it out.

I share with them that since my dad died I feel like my life is "Bare ruined choirs, where late the sweet birds sang." (*Sonnet 73*) This speaks volumes, and is more accurate than just saying I miss him. I inspire the basketball players with the famous St. Crispen's Day speech from Henry V: "But we in it shall be remembered—We few, we happy few, we band of brothers; For he who sheds his blood with me today shall be my brother;" and they are ready to run onto the field of play right then and there! Students are intrigued, and begin to make their own personal connections to… Shakespeare? Yes!

And there are reasons Shakespeare's words are so powerful and memorable. We must talk about the style of such poetry as this. For his writing is so smooth and so profound, it would be easy to overlook the parallel structure, imagery, alliteration, or metaphors, carefully crafted to create such effects on us, the readers. Yet the language is why we can relate, why we remember. There are countless other examples like these, the turn of a phrase, a quote, a title, and whole passages of great literature I can recall to mind in various situations. I want this for my students.

Now as an introduction, I will skip the lecture. Instead, I will have them locate, learn and recite their favorite lines from Shakespeare, because in their search they will learn enough background; and because recall is a valuable skill; and because reading the language of Shakespeare is valuable. The lessons of betrayal, ambition, love, selfishness, or pride will last as students remember the heroes of great literature, and how and why they fell. The lessons of language will last as they remember how and why it made them *feel*.

I do not feel that "literature is to the CCSS (Common Core State Standards) as dessert is to the food pyramid: Enjoy a little, but only when you can afford the calories and after you've finished your meal." (Callaghan, 2013) Independent reading may be "dessert" but literature study "offers students windows to other worlds, other cultures, other times. It poses intellectual challenges, demanding that students stretch and grow." (Jago, 2012) Not only is the sensory experience of reading books stimulating, it also has lasting affective and cognitive effects: "Dr. Oatley and Dr. Mar, in collaboration with several other scientists, reported in two studies, published in 2006 and 2009, that individuals who frequently read fiction seem to be better able to understand other people, empathize with them and see the world from their perspective." (Paul, 2012) Again, this is just further affirmation of what we who are readers already know. In fact, I recently read a novel that was so beautiful, so poignant, and so sad that I felt like it hurt my eyes to read it, but I couldn't stop reading it, either—like eating hot sauce, but in your soul and not your mouth.

As author Anne Lamott says, "Books help us understand who we are and how we are to behave." We should endeavor to equip our students with the skills, and instill in them the desire, to read literature. It is a gift they will cherish. We must be conscious not to abandon literature altogether as the pendulum swings now in the direction of informational, non-fiction, and expository text. The goal must be "to find balance: meet the needs of students by providing them opportunities for rich, meaningful experiences with a variety of texts." (Page, 2012) If we consider *why* we teach literature, including full-length novels, poetry, and the works of William Shakespeare, and make some adjustments in *how* we teach it, more students will come to understand and agree with the research: reading literature is, in fact, good for you.

There is no Frigate like a Book
To take us Lands away,
Nor any Coursers like a Page
Of prancing Poetry—
This Traverse may the poorest take
Without oppress of Toll—
How frugal is the Chariot
That bears a Human soul.

—Emily Dickenson

Notes and Reflection

CHAPTER THREE

READING NON-FICTION AND INFORMATIONAL TEXTS

"Journal of the Movement of the World: Stay centered without losing your shorts."

— Muriel Barbery, *The Elegance of the Hedgehog*

CHAPTER 3

READING NON-FICTION AND INFORMATIONAL TEXTS

There has been a shift in both the English Language Arts Common Core State Standards (CCSS) and the Texas Essential Knowledge and Skills (TEKS) standards in recent years to include increased emphasis on reading non-fiction and informational texts. "A close reading of the common core language arts standards reveals increased emphasis in each advancing grade on reading for the purpose of being able to 'do' and writing for the purpose of explaining to others." (Bartholomew, 2012) Indeed, one indicator of college readiness is the ability to read and interpret expository texts, and the current emphasis on these texts comes in part because we, and consequently our students, have been lacking in our preparation in these areas.

It has long been clear that reading boosts intelligence and expands vocabulary, and that our more successful students are readers. "Only in the past decade, however, have researchers begun to uncover that it's not just how much students read, that matters, but also what they read. In particular, students need to read and comprehend informational texts as often—and as fluently—as they do narrative texts." (Goodwin and Miller, 2013) Truly, informational, non-fiction, and digital texts represent a "journal of the movement of the world," and the ability to read, understand, and critique these various and sundry sub-genres will enrich and inform our students, and allow them to fully participate in the conversations happening around them.

For a long time I satisfied the curriculum requirements for non-fiction by just having my students read a couple of essays in the textbook. These were largely outdated historical treatises, and did not fire anybody up about the power and understanding that can be imparted and gained from writing and reading informational texts. Not surprisingly, non-fiction and informational text reading was my least favorite thing to teach. I may have even said something to my students like, "This is boring but we have to do it." (I know. Sigh.)

When I got serious about wanting to improve instruction, I realized I needed to find things my students wanted to read, that they would be reading in their lives outside of school; and I had to teach them how to read these things effectively. Indeed, to participate in many of the research-based responsive or personal writing tasks today, students must possess critical reading ability. "In addition to navigating digital information, students must understand informational text, as most sources on the internet are expository" (Pilgrim and Bledsoe, 2012). I began to incorporate informational texts in conjunction with teaching writing in the various modes. I taught students how to read them, and to use them as models to inform their own writing. As my awareness increased, I suddenly found non-fiction reading material, on topics my students and I were actually interested in, everywhere: in academic journals, magazines, newspapers, blogs, and online. Why, this wasn't boring at all!

I quickly realized, though, that simply replacing some of our curriculum material with new informational texts is not enough. We must teach students *how* to read non-fiction, which actually includes a vast array of sub-genres. Each sub-genre is unique and should be approached differently. Various genres are identifiable by not only their features, but their purposes. As their exposure grows, students will come to expect a "how-to" text to include graphics and numbered steps; and an editorial or blog to begin with a brief summary and include strong persuasive rhetoric. Understanding the features of different genres informs students' own writing. They begin to realize that in their academic and professional careers they will have to write for a variety of purposes and audiences, and the genre features and implications will dictate how and what they write.

Readers may sit down and get comfortable to read a novel. But to read a non-fiction essay, they first want to preview the text, examining the entire piece to see what is included and in what order; what is in bold or highlighted; what graphs and charts are present; what sources or hyperlinks are cited; and if the author is a credible source on the topic. They will need to underline main ideas, write notes in the margin, and circle certain words and phrases. They will need to re-read at times, and actively recall, paraphrase, connect, and apply throughout the process. We who are readers and scholars may take for granted the cognitive processes and skills for accessing these texts. For years it did not occur to me that in addition to motivating my secondary students and supplying them with interesting and diverse material to read, I would also need to teach them *how*.

Using real-world informational reading and writing assignments equips and empowers students and makes literacy relevant outside the classroom. Research suggests that while the ability to read and comprehend complex texts is a prediction of success after high school, the level of text complexity presented to students in school has actually decreased. And when they are assigned more complex texts, especially online, students rush through them: "Students often skimmed information to find quick answers or primarily attended to pictures and visuals." (Pilgrim and Bledsoe, 2012). This is characteristic of our culture: we want to get what we need as quickly as possible, and our students' reading habits reflect this.

It almost makes sense. But if all that was needed was a graphic, visual, or summary, why have the written text at all? The pictures are meant to supplement the real message, not substitute for it. "And in many high schools, teachers often don't even require students to read or comprehend these easier texts. Instead, many teachers attempt to make comprehension simpler for students by presenting material via power point or reading aloud." (Rothman, 2012) I find even my more advanced students will wait to see if I am going to tell them what the piece is about, or give them the key points in notes, rather than read it for themselves, protesting immediately that "it's too hard," or they "didn't understand," or "got lost." We must not be tricked into doing for them the most basic of our classroom survival skills.

Part of the process and reward of reading difficult text is rereading, paraphrasing, summarizing, and recalling, practices we must not only teach but insist on. Think of reading complex texts as comparable to a weight lifting workout. To get a good workout, you have to have the right amount of weight, which is just at the edge of your ability to lift.

Then, to build muscle over time, you have to increase the weights. The same is true for the level of reading material we give our students. Everything should not be instantly, easily accessible. There are some things worth a little effort to access.

Our students live in a "give up too quickly" age. When we jump in and summarize for them, we are sending the message to our students that the content is more important than the experience and skill of reading it for themselves. Our goal is to "build students capacity for independently comprehending a text through close reading." (Boyles) As teachers, we must be patient. When my nephew was three, he was trying to play a game on his grandmother's computer. My mom, ever helpful, was explaining to him repeatedly why he could not play that particular game in that way on her computer. He kept moving the mouse and squinting at the screen in concentration. She kept insisting he would not be able to do it that way. Finally, exasperated, he exclaimed, "If someone bees quiet, I can!!"

I think this is a good lesson to apply to reading instruction in our classrooms. Our inclination is to fill the uncomfortable silences in discussions about reading assignments with prompting, additional questions or hints, answers, or summaries, when to just be quiet would demand that students do the work themselves. We must not be too helpful, but push our students and allow them to reach their maximum reading capability.

I use short texts to teach students to read and comprehend non-fiction. I have known teachers to insist that students need to read long texts to prepare them for the length of the reading on standardized tests and college reading assignments. I keep a well-stocked classroom library of current full-length non-fiction, and my students enjoy our reader's choice unit with these texts. However, a runner training for a marathon rarely actually runs the entire distance. He runs intervals, or shorter distances. Short, current, informational texts lend themselves to discussion about issues, and students can formulate essential questions, offer different perspectives, and engage in higher level thinking skills, such as inference, connection, and application.

The teacher serves as a facilitator in these discussions, which can be organized to move out of the monologic, teacher-centered mode and into a circular, dialogic, student-centered model. Shorter texts allow students to have instruction and progress "through the entire sequence of a text" (Boyles), and repeat and retain the newly acquired skills. Reading complete shorter texts in a single class period can thus be very rewarding.

My students recently read a newspaper account on the collapse of a manufacturing building owned by U.S. companies in Bangladesh. They quickly moved to questions about accountability, and from there, to "How do we solve this problem without creating a bigger one?" They noted that to the people of Bangladesh, the potential to rise from abject poverty by working for pennies a day in this dangerous factory might be worth the risk. They wondered if the factories were closed because of unsafe working conditions, would the people in fact be worse off because they couldn't work at all. We read the song lyrics, "Are My Hands Clean," by Bernice Johnson Reagon in the same class period, and compared the language, style, and effects on readers of the two genres.

In another class, my students read a current short persuasive essay and discussed and responded to it. Then I had student groups each complete one of the following exercises: analyze the author's style and rhetorical choices using sentence stems; identify the thesis and write an outline of the writer's organizational method; explain several logical fallacies present in the article, such as post hoc and begging the question; and evaluate the sources and evidence mentioned, and credibility of the author. Each group used the document camera to share their work with the class. By using shorter texts, we are able to have a solid lesson resulting in learning and skill-improvement in just one class period.

It's such a struggle for the entire class when reading assignments, both literary and expository, include unfamiliar vocabulary. Students are unable to pronounce difficult words and unable to make meaning, and eventually they just give up, causing entire lessons to suffer. All of this can be avoided by donating a few minutes before reading to pre-teaching vocabulary. I first began to do this well into my career while teaching English Language Learners in my classroom. I soon discovered *all* students benefitted from it.

One of the things I teach my students when first approaching any reading assignment is to preview the text. This allows them to determine genre and purpose and look for graphics, headings, author information, sources cited, and other clues that will help them process the information. During this preview, students can scan and underline or circle any unfamiliar words. The teacher might also scan the material beforehand and make a list (instead of or in addition to having the students do this). The goal of any vocabulary study is for the words to become part of students' working vocabulary, not something they memorize for a quiz and then forget, which all teachers know is one of the pitfalls of vocabulary lessons. There are many ways to teach vocabulary to a class. Instead of giving students a list of the ten or twenty words we identify in the text that are unfamiliar, and having them define, write sentences, and memorize these for a quiz, I like to use various quick and engaging activities to teach the words.

A favorite vocabulary activity is "Show and Tell." I have each student choose one word from the text he or she has identified as unfamiliar. Students then announce which words they have chosen so we can avoid duplicates. Each student looks up the definition of his or her word, puts it into "student speak," and comes up with a way to demonstrate the word for the class. We all stand up. The first student says his word, defines it, and demonstrates it. The next student then has to say and act out the motion for the first student's word, and add his own new word. Each student repeats this action, by saying and acting out the previous word, and his own.

For example, when previewing the vocabulary in "Literacy Behind Bars," an excerpt from *The Autobiography of Malcolm X,* students identified words they didn't know as "vistas," "engrossing," and "penmanship." The student who had "vistas" said "a big, beautiful landscape view" and swept her arm about the room while exclaiming (with gusto): "VISTAS." The next student swept his arm about the room while saying "VISTAS"; and then announced "PENMANSHIP is good, careful, handwriting," and demonstrated this by pretending to carefully write something by hand. The third student said "PENMANSHIP" and pretended to write something by hand; and then said, "ENGROSSING describes something that is so interesting you are just totally absorbed in it and you can't look away." She put her face in the book and stared fixedly at it.

"Show and Tell" can be completed in large or small groups. At the end of the quick activity, I call out the words and the students all act out the motions associated with each of them. Then we read the article, and when students come across these words, they visualize them, understand them, and consequently, understand the text itself. Months later, I can call out "PENMANSHIP," and all students will pretend to write neatly in the air.

This activity helps my language learners more than anything I do, but I have found that when I introduce it like this, *all* students become more engaged in the reading and are more enthusiastic about learning new vocabulary. The benefits to pre-teaching vocabulary outweigh the costs (the time it takes). Teachers are so excited in my workshops when we model "Show and Tell" because they know it will work. Like me, they wonder why they didn't think of something like this sooner. Relevance is obvious and retention increases tenfold with the kinesthetic and visual elements of the activity.

After students have previewed the text, and become familiar with new vocabulary, they will begin to read. As they read, have them interact with the text and ask themselves throughout the process: What just happened? What is the point? What does that mean to me? They can do this by underlining the most important sentence in each paragraph, or by writing key words in margins. This kind of close reading requires time to stop and actively recall what was in a paragraph or on a page. It doesn't matter how many times students reread material; unless active recall is used, it is unlikely they will remember the "gist" or key points in the article. (How many times have we heard, "But I read it six times and still failed the quiz!")

Upon conclusion of reading, students should use their active recall skills, notes, and highlighting to write a summary, the length of which is determined by the length of the original piece. A three or four page non-fiction article might be summarized in 5-8 sentences. I teach them the difference in the main idea or message, and an actual summary: a summary of the writing includes the details and the supporting points for the message. Students need summary skills for their college days, certainly, but also for careers and for life. Law enforcement officers write police reports, lawyers write briefs, doctors write medical reports, and scientists report findings. All of these are summaries. Any reading assignment, or students' own essays, can be summarized in class. Paraphrasing is the "first step along the journey to close reading. If students can't paraphrase the basic content of a passage, how can they dig for its deeper meaning?" (Boyles)

Our students lack paraphrasing and summarizing skills because we do it for them. Consider what happens in many math classes where the teachers are so helpful. The students read a word problem and ask the teacher, "What is it asking us to do?" The teacher, thinking she is not actually giving them the answer to the *math* part of the problem, will paraphrase the question. The students then ask, "Well, how do we do that?" and the teacher explains the steps needed to reach the answer, because after all, she is not *doing* it for them. Then the students perform poorly on the math assessments, and the teacher insists, "They could do it in class!" Could they?

In English class, where reading is the most basic of building block skills, we must not succumb to the urge to do it for them, to paraphrase, to give them the content and then test them on content. I constantly have to remind myself of this. We must teach students to *access the content for themselves.* That is the skill, the standard. The content is, in fact, secondary. Truly, our assessments should test the *skills* of reading, paraphrasing, and summarizing new material.

In addition to summarizing, I also have students respond to non-fiction by making connections. The responses may be personal, and should connect the big ideas in the reading to something in life or something else they have read. The literary response must show me that they have synthesized and internalized the information and can transfer and apply it. This personal connection must not become more important than comprehension; rather it is based on accurate understanding and representation of the text.

In fact, one of the areas in which students struggle on assessments is the ability to correctly select and use text evidence. So, teachers may require that student responses include a minimum of two or more references to text, one directly quoted and the other paraphrased, from different parts of the article or story, that serve to develop and support the points the students are making. This requirement encourages them to read for themselves instead of just listening to a discussion or asking someone about the piece, and trying to formulate a response from what others say. It also facilitates active engagement with the text during the reading since they have to identify points along the way which they want to address in their responses.

A significant component of reading both fiction and non-fiction, and arguably the most neglected and most important in a true writing class, is the analysis. In *Two Roads Diverged and I Took Both: Meaningful Writing Instruction in an Age of Testing*, I proposed teaching writing from classroom reading we are already using. One of the trainings I offer for teachers in which we model this process is called "Reading Like a Writer." My point is, as English teachers, we need to get back in the kitchen and focus our classroom instruction on how good writing is created. It is not enough to simply say during or after reading a book or selection, "Wow, this is good." We need to examine the recipe with our students through analysis of the author's specific structure and style.

We have for so long spent so much time on historical and author background, setting, theme, plot outlines, literary elements, characterization, ethics, philosophy, and content that we have neglected the very brick and mortar of a writing classroom: the writing itself. We must take note of the craft of writing: the writer's choices, his or her stylistic and rhetorical decisions and the effects of these on readers. Informational texts provide an excellent platform for a proactive study of the art and science of writing through which we can and should teach our students to *read like a writer, and write for a reader*, and thus, fully immerse themselves in the conversations of literacy happening around them.

Summary and response do not pose the level of difficulty for students that analysis does, because analysis is rooted in prior knowledge of grammar, rhetoric, style, academic vocabulary, and critical thought. Our students aren't used to "reading like a writer." But we can teach them to do so, when we begin to integrate reading and writing lessons. The new Texas reading assessments support this practice. Most of the questions on the reading test are actually about the writer's choices, and not the content of the selections. This question was on the first administration of a new Texas state assessment test given to 9th graders, after they were instructed to read a blog:

"How does the writer's approach to the topic make it accessible to the reader?"

Students were widely unsuccessful, primarily because the language is not in "student-speak," as I call it. Without intervention—known as teaching—my students were at a loss to answer this question. I wrote it on my white board and left it all year. We answered it for every single thing we read in class: poetry, fiction, persuasive writing, expository writing, drama, and even student handbooks and course information. After we had talked about the content of our reading I simply asked students if they thought it was easy to understand, if they enjoyed it, or if they were moved or motivated by it. Then I asked them what specifically the author did that caused their reaction to the reading. What made it work?

For example, I gave my seniors an article to read about studying for college exams. After we talked about the content, which certainly was helpful, I directed their attention to how it was presented. I asked them if the piece was well-written. They agreed that it was easy for them to understand and remember. Why? One student noted that the use of "First," "Second," and "Third," helped her identify the main steps to studying. Another said the use of "you" by the author made her feel as if he was speaking directly to her, giving her advice. A third pointed out that short paragraphs were more accessible than big chunks of text on a page. All of these, my students now know, are stylistic choices made by a writer to make his information accessible to readers.

I have the students present their comments using sentence stems: "The author uses _____ to _____. This shows the readers _____." Or "The author uses _____ such as (text evidence) _____ to _____."

Students might say, "The author uses second person to establish an instructive yet friendly tone with the reader.

This shows that it is an advice essay." Or: "The author uses short paragraphs to make her points about how to study. This actually mimics how you should study: review short chunks of information. This is easier than reading or studying it all at once." Students can do this, and it's enjoyable. I have them work in pairs, or groups; then we share with the whole class.

I have had English teachers in my trainings work a good twenty minutes on one sentence stem. "This is hard!" they exclaim. "I know what the writer is doing but it's hard to put it into words!" But that is the point: we *have* to put it into words, and into academic, critical writing. It's easy to let students just tell each other, or pretend to tell each other. It's also fairly easy to *identify* rhetoric but not understand its purpose or effectiveness. The academic language and specificity of sentence stems truly holds students accountable for the learning goal, which is a close analysis of the distinct qualities and effectiveness of a writer's style.

To introduce them to and set the expectation for this type of academic language and study, teachers might begin with six word memoirs (Google it!), even the first day of school:

"Moving again. Goodbye, strangers. Hello, strangers."

Students use the sentence stems provided to think about and articulate the choices made by the writer:

"**The author uses** the repetition of the word strangers **to show that** she never has any friends, because she is never in a place long enough to make them."

"**The author uses** short sentences **to emphasize** the brevity of her stay in each place she lived, and to create a depressing tone."

"Leap! Catch football. Crunch. Goodbye scholarship."

"**The author uses** onomatopoeia in the word 'crunch' **to emphasize** the devastation of the injury."

"**The author uses** the positive tone word 'Leap!' with exclamation point **to** start the reader off feeling exhilarated, so the rest of the story has more impact."

From analysis activities like these, even with the shortest of texts, students learn to talk in academic language and think about and write about author style. Later in the year these sentence stems come naturally to them in their own discussions. These activities help students who struggle to answer open-ended response questions on reading tests. They are appropriate for struggling learners and gifted learners. They also prompt students to *think about their own readers when they write*. So this question, "How does the writer's approach to the topic make it accessible to the reader," though so daunting at first, actually ended up being one of the single most effective teaching tools I had all year, resulting in sustainable, measurable skills in reading, speaking, and writing, for all levels of students.

To see how teaching these close-reading skills, such as preview, summary, response, inference, transfer, connection, and analysis, with non-fiction text might look in a classroom lesson, consider the following examples. (Teachers may substitute any grade-level appropriate, interesting essays for the one in this example.)

My high school students read Anna Quindlen's "All My Babies Are Gone Now." This is a humorous and poignant first person narrative reflection of the worries and blessings of parenting, by a mother after her children are grown and gone. In it she reflects that perhaps she rushed through their childhood, trying so hard to get it right and get it done, and now she longs to treasure those little moments again. This, she realizes, is the real lesson of parenting.

After students read it, I have them discuss it in small groups. I tell my students that everything written is part of a larger conversation, and when they read, they are participating in the conversation. In small group discussions students are forming their responses, discovering what they will bring to the conversation. Sometimes I have them write first, and discuss second. The benefit to this is that there will be those students who think of something totally different than anyone else's response, and brilliant, yet they may be hesitant to share initially, or just listening to everyone else talk may sway them to think the same way and go down the same avenues. I like the risk-taking of having them write first.

But other times, we discuss first, which also has benefits: it gives them more to think about than just their own ideas; and as they begin to listen and think about what classmates offer, perhaps there is a line of thinking that they, too, relate to, or can develop, that they would not have thought of without the conversation. This also helps struggling learners, language learners, and shy students, to gain confidence in their ideas and to understand difficult text through listening to "student speak" about it. Regardless, students need to have a written response, to learn to articulate and connect their thoughts, just as a written summary requires them to read closely and paraphrase accurately. Teachers can set the guidelines for length, text evidence, and so on. I generally model for students the first few times we write an **SRA** (Summary, Response, Analysis), and share my own responses.

This was the response I shared with students after reading "All My Babies Are Gone Now."

> When she was little, I was my niece's favorite person. I was first on the birthday guest list, no matter how many miles separated us at the time. 'Who do you want to come to your birthday party?' her mother (my sister) asked her. She was about six. 'Well,' she said seriously, 'There's Omie' (that's me), 'and, well, Omie, and…well, just Omie, really.' I was the cool aunt.
>
> She packed her 'night-night' and toothbrush and had sleepovers with me from the time she was three

years old. We talked on the phone. I was her 'BFF,' she told me on more than one occasion. Now, I rarely see my niece, who is almost twenty-one, and never talk to her, because even when she is here she has headphones on, or is texting, with Omie right there in the same room.

I used to talk to my nephew about cars and football. When he was two years old, he could talk pretty good and had a really deep voice, like a teenager, but he could not pronounce 'tr.' He pronounced 'tr' as f. So train was fain, and trike was fike. And of course he loved more than anything, **tr**ucks. So every time we went anywhere, he would see trucks—real ones, toy ones, pick-ups, or 18-wheelers—and scream, 'Trrruccckk, Omie, Truck!!' Except with an 'F.' I pulled away from Whataburger once without paying when a large truck came rolling down the high way in the distance and I saw his little eyes squinting, then lighting up, and his chest inhale with that deep breath he was about to use to shout, 'TRUCK, Omie,' but with an F. We would wrestle, and he would drive my golf cart, and he, too, thought I was the bomb. Last week, I had a thirty minute conversation with this nephew about why he could not drop out of school at seventeen, why everyone in the world was not a faker, and why just because marijuana grows in the ground, does not mean God has ordained it to be the best and safest drug of all and we should all smoke it to relax. I still am stunned from this conversation.

I miss these kids. And they are right here. But the main thing this article makes me think of is the loss of my dad. Because the message to me is as Quindlen stated: treasure the doing it and not the getting it done. How I wish I could wash the boat for my dad one more time. And there are a thousand other wishes just like that. I did so many things to get them done. And now they are done, and I would give years off my life to be doing them, with him, again.

Do not be afraid to share your responses with students from time to time. Let them see you are human and vulnerable, and that revealing this is often what makes our writing powerful, and meaningful to others. Let them see reading and writing inspire you.

After students have summarized and responded to an essay, such as "All My Babies Are Gone Now," it is time for the analysis of style *("How does the writer's approach to the topic make it accessible to the reader?")*

Students are instructed to re-read the essay and examine the author's stylistic, rhetorical, or grammatical choices. It is important to have good group conversations about style, especially early in the year, modeling analysis with everything students read. I also suggest having some reminder key-words for style analysis on the walls, posters, or posts on the web students can readily access. These key words might include diction, dialect, sentence structure, paragraph structure, rhetorical questions, parallelism, repetition, juxtaposition, allusion, anecdote, figurative language, point of view, use of unconventional grammar, (parenthetical statements or fragments), or grammatical techniques like the dash, semi-coon, or colon. Students also have sentence stems to help them get started.

Here is the quick in-class analysis I modeled and shared with students:

> In 'All My Babies Are Gone Now,' Anna Quindlen's stylistic devices make her essay easily accessible and enjoyable to readers. She uses short sentences: 'All my babies are gone now.' Later, 'no one knows anything.' 'Last year he went to China. Next year he goes to college. He can talk just fine. He can walk, too.' These short sentences are like years passing. She uses fragments the same way: 'The nightmare sleepover. The horrible summer camp.' This shows the reader that events, years, are piling up in the past tense pile. They went quickly, and are gone in a blink.
>
> The author uses rhetorical questions (Par 8) to show what a mother goes through, that you constantly question yourself. It doesn't matter what the questions are; moms all wonder if they are doing everything right. She uses humor, which always resonates with an audience, making fun of all the things she did wrong according to her children. All parents can relate to having their children tell them how they screwed up in so many ways—or if not a

parent, a child can relate because we have told our parents: remember when you made me sit at the table for six hours because I would not take a 'thank you bite' of spinach? Her specific examples of doctors and books make her experiences more realistic and credible. She backs up what she says with examples that most parents—and children—will relate to, which bring a smile and a subconscious 'Oh, yeah!'

Quindlen uses interesting grammar: the colon, for lists; the dash, for after thoughts. The parenthetical statements when her kids wanted her to include things, which made it more real for readers, like she was letting us in on a secret. She uses lists and repetition, and parallel structure, such as in the third sentence: 'Three people who read…who tell…who want…' In fact, her use of the fragment in paragraph 2 works because it is continuing the parallel structure established in the previous paragraph.

I like her style. It is journalistic, so it is not surprising to learn that she has a newspaper background, yet it's poignant at the same time. And I love her theme, or message, which allows all readers to relate, whether they are parents or not: treasure the doing it and not the getting it done.

Allow students time to talk about your analysis and theirs, and to make notes to which they may refer later on the next assignment. As you point out the various stylistic techniques, have students try some short writing exercises using them. For example, after reading Quindlen's essay, they can try to write using parenthesis, items in a series, fragments for emphasis, and rhetorical questions. (They love this last one: "Does my English teacher not know I have six other classes? Does she think I enjoy homework? Does she not understand that I have a basketball game? Is she crazy?") Ask students which of these techniques they see themselves incorporating successfully into their own writing.

There are other reading and writing skills to be taught from any assigned reading. Since inference is not only a critical life skill, but an assessed standard at almost every grade level, I would ask students what they can infer from the article. They should back up their inferences with text evidence. Some may say that the author's children are successful, and that they have a good relationship. Others offer that they can tell by her references to specific books on parenting that she is educated. Still others say they can infer that the books she read on parenting really didn't help her that much.

We talk about how students were able to transfer her message even though they are children and not parents; how they were able to make meaning for themselves and enjoy the piece from perhaps a different perspective. We have an in-depth grammar lesson, usually lasting an entire class period, on this essay. I point out to students how Quindlen uses a colon, a dash, a list, fragments, and parentheses, and have them practice them in their own writing. Something that is hard to teach students (and is always assessed on standardized tests) is parallelism; this essay provides excellent examples for students to study and model. The depth, breadth, and scope of study that can come from short informational texts is remarkable.

Finally, we can connect the topics, tones and themes of the essays and articles we read to different genres. With Quindlen's essay I might pair poems such as "Those Winter Sundays" by Robert Hayden or "My Papa's Waltz" by Theodore Roethke. In the former, the speaker is the adult child, reflecting on how he took for granted his father's quiet acts of love. In Roethke's poem, the speaker is also the adult child, remembering dancing with his father, who was quite probably intoxicated. Both poems offer so much for students to discuss, not just in comparison with the essay, but about how the elements of poetry create tone and contribute to theme, much like the elements of style contributed to Quindlen's message in the essay.

This is not just one essay and two poems that can be taught this way. Whatever the grade level, there are informational, narrative, non-fiction texts that interest students, and there's a poem that can be connected. An excerpt from Malcolm X's Autobiography, "Literacy Behind Bars," has been especially inspiring for both my adult community college students and my high school students. After reading, students respond, often expressing guilt that they take their education, specifically their ability and opportunity to read and write, for granted. This essay inspires them, at least temporarily, to approach studies more seriously.

I have students summarize the essay; then I have them compare summaries with others in their group, and write group summaries to share with the class. I have them analyze the style. Most students note the specific examples from the dictionary (Aardvark), the short paragraphs, and the imagery of reading by the light under the cell door. Recent student analyses (with sentence stems, since this was the very first such reading and analysis we did in the course) included the following comments:

> **The author uses** great diction, such as 'feigned,' 'vistas,' and 'engrossing,' **to** stop his readers in their tracks by confronting them with a workout for their vocabulary. Replacing overused words with colorful synonyms prevents the reader from becoming bored with the text.

> **The author uses** great description of the prison. He puts you there, 'reading in that glow.' You can visualize him sitting on the floor and then jumping up and into bed when he heard the guard.

My students infer that the speaker had it rough and grew up on the streets, and that he is proud of his education. I ask them to transfer their learning: What is *your* literacy narrative? What did you have to really work at, of which you are especially proud?

With this selection from Malcolm X's autobiography, I pair Pablo Neruda's poem, "Poetry." In it the speaker believes he truly came alive when he discovered poetry—or rather, it discovered him—much like Malcolm feels he did when he learned to read and write. "I did not know what to say,/ my mouth had no way with names,/ my eyes were blind,/ and something started in my soul…" Students easily make the connection between the two genres, and discuss topics for their own writing, perhaps things they "discovered" that changed them thereafter. We also compare the optimistic tone of Malcolm's recounting of his prison experience to that in Maya Angelou's poem, "Still I Rise," and discuss overcoming hardship as another topic for students to explore in their own writing.

There are many more examples I could share of essays and poems I use together to teach critical reading and writing, because the content is not what is important; the skills are. If we teach in this way, connections are readily apparent to students when they take assessment tests that require them to connect across genres. I also believe we empower them to see connections and make comparisons more readily in life outside school. When I get ready to assess my students, I can give them an essay to read, and ask them to write an "SRA" (Summary, Response, Analysis), or make connections between pieces, or answer (or create) questions about inference, transfer, topic, tone, theme, and style—and they can do this. And the analysis of style never gets boring, just as golf never gets boring, because just as every course, every day, and every shot is different, so is everything we read. Every analysis is a fresh look at how writers do it.

"How does the writer's approach to the topic make it accessible to the reader?" Being able to answer that question not only helps students be better and more aware readers, it helps them be better and more aware writers as well. Reading, connecting, and recognizing information, messages and themes in literature and media, are life skills that will enrich and serve our students well beyond the classroom. I feel almost like I am choosing Christmas gifts for my family when I choose what to give my students to read. It is that important to me to get it right.

At the close of each semester, I ask my students to reflect on their experiences with reading and writing and English class in general over the last year. Here are a few of the reflections I received recently, that reinforce and reaffirm the instructional strategies in this chapter.

Student Reflections

"I have grown the most through becoming a better writer. I learned to write, from reading a lot."

"This year I have connected to my own abilities as a writer. Our work with stories and essays has furthered my own writing so much. I believe that to be a good writer, you must be a good reader—and that is what this class has taught me to be."

"I think that I will remember most that being challenged is actually the way that you learn. I have learned so much in English this year."

"I know my style will change some more since I'm only seventeen after all, but before this class, I don't think I really had a style at all."

"The more attentive you are when you read, the more you can learn and truly relate it to real life. Now I know what I've been missing out on. P.S. I read books for fun now."

Perhaps there is a *Promised Land* after all. Milk and honey, colleagues. Milk and honey.

Notes and Reflection

CHAPTER FOUR

HOW TO REALLY TEACH WRITING

"There is nothing to writing. All you do is sit down at a typewriter and bleed."

—Ernest Hemingway

CHAPTER 4

HOW TO REALLY TEACH WRITING

Any time I am told something along the lines of "Here's a computer; go make a web page," I freak out just a little bit. It's like "Some assembly required," or "Easy directions included." I don't know what the parts are called; I don't have the tools or understand the language; and I end up with bookcase shelves in upside down. This is not unlike saying to a student, "Here's a topic; go make an essay." We must actively teach our students how to write.

In much the same way a coach teaches athletes to play a game, this involves teaching the fundamentals, as well as strategy. It involves preparing for various situations. Without proper instruction in dribbling, passing, lay-ups, and defensive techniques, a basketball scrimmage would be a nightmare to watch. If players didn't know their roles on the team, the boundaries, the goals, and the rules, and had not prepared for various situations or teams they may encounter, the game would not be a success for anyone involved. So doomed is a writing assignment lacking proper instruction in fundamentals of grammar, purpose, and style.

So where do we start? We first may teach students how to write by teaching them how parts of sentences and paragraphs function. I do not do this with a grammar book, because what I have learned while teaching suggests that students do not retain information they have underlined in a grammar book. Nor do they make any connection from circling correct verbs or drawing arrows to modifiers, to their own writing or to their lives outside the classroom. Students can repeatedly underline the participial phrase in a sentence and draw an arrow to the word it modifies. They do not know why they are doing it and fail to make any connection to writing from this meaningless activity. But for years I, along with many other ELA teachers I am sure, just did not know a better way. And we have to teach grammar. Grammar is the GPS of writing, the directions for when to go up and down or pause or stop. It is akin to road signs, without which we would drive in chaos. It is the power that allows our students to make meaning for their readers.

Consider the sentence: "A woman, without her man, is nothing." This would be very different if we punctuated it differently: "A woman: without her, man is nothing." Aside from just providing clarity, Standard Academic English can open doors for students. One way I teach grammar so that students can understand how it can impact their writing is through what I call "Creative Grammar Lessons."

To begin a lesson on participles, I tell students that participles are "ing" words that look like verbs but act like adjectives in the sentence. I show them sample sentences with participles and participial phrases, and point out what purpose they serve and how they add to a sentence. Then I ask students to write their own boring sentences. We might start with something like this: "The boy sat at the desk." I ask students to add "ing" words that look like verbs but act like adjectives, to the beginning or end of the sentence, to paint a better picture for the readers. Recent student examples were: "Fidgeting and scowling, the boy sat at the desk." "The boy sat at the creaking, crumbling, confining desk." And one overachiever used participles at the beginning and end of his sentence: "Hoping and praying, the boy sat at the desk, dreaming that he was on the winning team."

When students are ready for independent practice, I ask them to write their own starter sentences about something that happened yesterday, either at home or at school. Students love to write and share about their own lives. This is so much more fun than reading boring sentences in a grammar workbook. An easy way to allow all students to share is simply to have them pair-share, "turn to a neighbor," or if they are sitting at tables, share with the group. These quick shares allow students to all get to have a voice in a fraction of the time. I then ask for volunteers, or draw from my playing cards I keep with all students' names on them, to choose someone to share aloud.

On one such occasion, Ricky (not his real name), one of the more struggling (albeit more eager) learners in my classroom, volunteered and read his sentence: "I watched my dad leave the family." That is another chapter in itself, isn't it? These moments are lessons in perspective. Here I am trying to teach participles to this child, and his dad left. I am reminded of the blessing it is to be an English teacher, for certainly he would not have had opportunity to share his heart in a class where reading and writing activities were not the primary focus. ("$3x + 9 = 18$, and by the way, my dad left?")

I told Ricky that I was so sorry he was going through that, and that his sentence had real potential to express his emotions, and I thanked him for sharing. Other students shared their sentences as well. Then I instructed the class to add "ing" words—participles or participial phrases—to paint a more specific picture for the reader. And this was Ricky's sentence (his spelling):

"Sadening, frustrating, awakening, I watched my dad leave the family, peeling away from my life."

After a moment of hushed nervousness, students began exclaiming: "Dude, that sucks." "Man, that's rough." "My dad left last year so I know how you feel." "That was a really good sentence." And so on. And Ricky, not a popular kid at all, felt like someone cared about what he was going through, and he wasn't alone. His peers sympathized with his experience. And when I said, "Who wants to share next?" another student blurted, "I'm not going after that!" Ricky sat up a little straighter in his chair and grinned. You see, no one had ever said that about him before. He felt validated, academically and personally, from a grammar lesson. This empathy and affirmation does not happen from underlining participial phrases in a book or on a worksheet. It happened in the classroom that day because we wrote about our lives and used the participles to clarify, identify, elaborate, and describe.

But the cognitive effects of the lesson, the primary purpose, were lasting, too. The next time we wrote essays, before my students submitted them, I stopped them: "Hey, remember when we did that lesson on participles last week?"

Collectively: "Nooooo." (Of course. Don't you love them?)

"Yes, you do. The 'ing' words?"

"Oh, yeah, yeah."

"Well, go back in your essays and see if there are places you could add participles or participial phrases, to really describe something and paint a better picture for the reader." They could and did. And the next time we wrote essays, some remembered and did this without my prompting, during the writing process. A grammar lesson that transferred to writing! Don't say!

I have students do the same types of activities for many different components of grammar and style. During one such lesson, students write with subordinating conjunctions to express an opinion about something we read in class:

"Although he lived in the woods, Thoreau was not really a hermit."

"If Emily Dickenson were alive today, we would probably be friends."

"Unless I give up my cell phone, I cannot call myself a transcendentalist."

We have to teach students how to build sentences and to vary sentence structure. This helps their writing and my sanity, because I get tired of reading the barest, shortest, most boring sentences for every assignment or test on which they have to "write a complete sentence." I teach students to combine sentences with semi-colons "to instantly look smarter," as one student said. I have them think of and practice using words that indicate examples are coming ("for example," "specifically," "consider"); or words that indicate we are switching to a new topic ("however," "on the other hand"); or words that indicate we are wrapping up and heading to the final stretch or conclusion ("finally," "therefore," "as a result"). I have them text something, and then translate it into academic language; or take a poem with little punctuation and write it as a paragraph. I show them how the various ways they punctuate these things can change the meaning completely.

These grammar lessons become a game for students in which they try to out-do each other, as was the case on the day I instructed them to write a sentence about a novel we were reading, *The Secret Life of Bees*. One witty young man wrote: "I almost turned into a girl while reading *The Secret Life of Bees*." I then instructed the class to add a subordinate clause at the beginning of the sentence. He wrote: **"Although I enjoyed it**, I almost turned into a girl while reading *The Secret Life of Bees*." Add a prepositional phrase: "Although I enjoyed it, I almost turned into a girl, **with tears and temper tantrums,** while reading *The Secret Life of Bees*." And finally, add an appositive clause: "Although I, **a manly man,** enjoyed it, I almost turned into a girl, with tears and temper tantrums, while reading *The Secret Life of Bees*." If we can laugh during learning, better yet.

I want my students to learn that grammar is like musical notations; we need it to tell us how to play the song. Without it, everything is open to interpretation and confusion. We should require everything presented in class on a power point, media presentation, video, short answer question, or test to be grammatically correct. Holding students accountable will cause retention and real learning. If we don't, we are sending the message that what we do for a living doesn't matter, and how they write really doesn't matter even though we spend instructional time on it. That's like attending staff development training on something you are never going to apply, and no one wants to do that.

I teach grammar and punctuation by having students frequently write paragraphs: In today's paragraph, use a semi-colon. Use a dependent clause. Use a participle. Use proper nouns. This is easily incorporated into short writing tasks and makes for more purposeful journaling as well. Have students free write (I much prefer "purposefully" write) for five minutes on a prompt at the beginning of class if you want to, but include a review of skills you recently taught, such as: "And include three prepositional phrases, and one powerful verb."

I recently saw a cute poster: "Let's eat Grandma! (Grammar Saves Lives!)" Obviously there should be a comma: "Let's eat, Grandma." We have beauty and meaning and order in language because we have grammar. What I learned about grammar through years of teaching it, is that correct use of participles, parts of speech, punctuation, spelling, and style is a value. We cannot suit up and play the game without these fundamental skills. The method—the way we get students to learn, retain, recall, and use the information forever—is a choice. With a little careful planning and intentional instruction, my students' beliefs about and use of Standard Academic English, and consequently, their writing, improved.

I also teach students a basic structure, or formula for success, to memorize and use when they are in a bind and need to write a paragraph or essay. Obviously the exact length and style will vary depending on the writing situation, such as purpose, space allotted, specific instructions, and more. But giving them some basic tools, especially for expository writing, keeps them from panicking. Students use formulas for math all the time. I memorized percentages as a kid and now know exactly how much those shoes, at 30% off, will cost. I want my students to have the same kind of knowledge base for various writing tasks that arise during their lives. The structure and process I teach them can be modified for various purposes, grades, and ability levels.

I first model for students the pre-writing process. Here is your topic; what do you want to say about it? Think of everything you know and everything you've done related to the topic. Generate all your experiences and beliefs about it, and then organize it according to purpose. For example, if the topic is walls, students can write an expository piece explaining how walls are beneficial and serve a purpose. Expository = explain. They may want to write a narrative piece about walls they have encountered or constructed in their own lives. Narrate = tell a story. Students can write a persuasive piece about tearing down or constructing walls.

If the topic is change, ask students what they think about change. What are all the various causes, effects, benefits, and obstacles to change? Tell them if they explain their opinions on change, using examples from history, literature, politics, life, and their own experiences, this is expository writing. If they attempt to convince someone they love to change something, this is persuasive writing. They may write a story about a young person who was forced to change his or her beliefs (literary), or about their own experiences with change (narrative). The purpose dictates the organization, form, tone, and style the essay takes.

Once we have a topic and ideas, we must generate a thesis statement and begin planning. During the prewriting process of the essay, divide the paper in half. On one side, put one main idea about your thesis, and on the other, put another main idea or point about your thesis. I explain that these are the paragraphs, and that every paragraph has a main point to make supporting the thesis. For each point, students will need facts and examples, which may be supported with text evidence, research or elaboration. So, we list two or three good facts or examples in support of each point. Then I tell them each fact must be explained, and connections made for the reader. And all this can be ordered: Topic sentence, fact, two or three elaborations, fact, two or three elaborations, concluding sentence.

For example, if I am writing about change, and I have decided to persuade others to change their habits to preserve the environment, my thesis might be: "There are things humans must do, individually and collectively, in their lives and practices to decrease the damaging effects to nature and the environment in which we live." My prewriting organization/ideas might look like this:

Body 1
Main point for this paragraph: **individuals.**

Point 1: Use bikes, or carpool when possible. Talk about effects of emissions, smog, auto pollution, and the benefits of carpooling or walking. List these here, with research.

Point 2: Talk about using plastic bags, refilling water bottles, and not littering while boating, driving, or eating outside. Show why it should matter to us all. Use dolphin example and pictures.

Body 2
Main point for this paragraph: **government.**

Point 1: Talk about steps already taken by govt. to help and show that they work: ethanol, wind generators, smoking ban. Provide research.

Point 2: Talk about steps the govt. still needs to take, such as prohibiting plastic bags at convenience stores (take your own), promoting clean drinking water without bottles, and cracking down on boaters who litter or drive through sea grass with props down.

Ideas for both: use graphics or visuals and hyperlinks to engaging video clips for emotional appeal. Put in a chart of statistics.

The above prewriting allows students then to organize the paragraphs easily. I call it building the essay. For timed assessments on which many students don't have time or won't take time to write full drafts and revise them, prewriting like this is invaluable. They can write all the pieces in detail and then just transfer them to the actual essay answer sheet, revising and editing as they transfer. For students who will have weeks to write several drafts, this prewriting gives them a solid foundation on which to build. Tip: remind students to conclude each paragraph and transition into the next, as this is something they often forget. We talk about and practice transitions as one of our essential building blocks of writing. The first things students should think when they approach a writing assignment is "What do I want to say and how best can I get my point across to readers?" not "How long do you want it to be?" If they understand pre-writing and know a basic structure for organizing their essays, their passion and purpose will dictate the length, style, and tone.

Teaching academic writing is hard work. It would be much easier to just let students write creatively in journals, discuss texts and their thoughts about them aloud, or write short fragmented answers about content on tests. It is hard work to create meaningful, academic writing assignments and go over them piece by painstaking piece, instructing, modeling, providing feedback, and promoting growth. Yet academic, critical, responsive writing is an essential skill. "Critical writing creates meaning, solidifies connections, transforms subconscious ideas into conscious thoughts, and is essential for authentic literacy." (Cain and Laird, 2011)

I agree with Peg Tyre: Most kids who graduate from high school are not going to be creative writers—so why is so much time spent on this kind of writing instead of organized, structured, purposeful writing? Indeed, over the years I have seen enrichment activities that go along with novels that are fun to do but not enriching anything at all. For example, after reading *The Secret Life of Bees,* instead of writing journal entries from a character's perspective we ought to be teaching students to write about the three references in the novel to events that most define the time, or had the greatest impact on culture and history.

Students could write a one page document, citing text evidence from both the novel and outside sources, and include links to video clips of the events they reference—a component of new literacy that makes writing interactive, enrichment and extension relevant, and reading engaging. Instead of building a model of the Globe Theater or writing a plot outline of *Macbeth*, students could discuss how Shakespeare's use of clothing imagery propels the plot forward and further enhances understanding of the theme.

Making a list in response to a prompt or question is easy. Telling a neighbor or free-writing in a journal is easy. Students should be required to write their thoughts in solid, well-developed sentences, and organize them into paragraphs. This helps students get used to writing academically within the confines of space and time. Teachers constantly ask me for help in teaching students to write short, open-ended responses on state assessment tests. If students were consistently required to write acceptable, critical, academic short answers with text evidence during the course of a regular school day or week, this would not be an area of weakness. This should be a regular and frequent expectation in all classes, regardless of subject area.

Teachers used to have reservations about allowing students to use word processors with spell checkers and grammar aids enabled; now we beg them to use these tools. We used to warn against even thinking about Wikipedia; now it is generally agreed that it is not a bad place to begin a search. Today's young writers are social; while they may not have a notebook handy to write in at all times, they will have a cell phone or tablet or computer. They can read, write, email, or text material from almost anywhere. "This [passing notes] has been replaced by another 'not-on-task' behavior, texting, another literate behavior we could tap for our own educational purposes; students could 'text' to their blog or their online writer's notebook." (Strickland, 2009) While the debate about technological devices in the classroom continues, a wait-and-see approach has served me best.

In my dual credit 12th grade English class recently, two boys used their phones for everything. Neither could keep up with books or papers. At first I constantly walked by their work stations to ensure they were on task and not texting or playing games. Then I decided that they were apparently compensating for lack of organizational skills. Rather than miss the lesson because they could not keep up with handouts, notes, books, or paper, they kept it all on the cell phone, a device that was always in their pockets! There they could access stories and handouts I distributed or posted, take classroom notes, or write. They sent the writing to me if I requested it, or to themselves to retrieve later. When I asked one to share an in-class written response to a complex and controversial essay we had read, he stood up and read his articulate and intriguing attack right from his phone.

I realize these students' ingenuity should be applauded, not prohibited. I mistakenly thought they were compensating for a lack of organization or responsibility, but they weren't lacking anything at all. They were organized. They were reading, thinking, and writing. *It just looked different.* Perhaps the period of adjustment, the learning curve, is mine. I have learned that what we often criticize in today's students are not faults; they are differences. They complete almost every task we give them differently than previous generations did. That doesn't make them wrong. Some of my students today are more comfortable "writing" on their phones than they are writing on paper. They use these phones to write correctly and beautifully; to write poems and store research documents. If students check their Facebook page, or text once or twice during class, is that so different than all the doodling I did in the margin of notebooks when I was a student? I can still teach today's students how to write well. They have taught me, then, to let them.

An important part of the writing process is revision. Writers have always known revision was the most important and time-consuming part of the entire writing process. But our students don't want to do it. Ask them to revise and they will copy the first draft of an essay word for word, and possibly correct a spelling or comma mistake. Our students don't realize what a wonderful thing revision is! They need to "revise" their thinking of revision. In golf, a mulligan is a do-over, a second chance to hit the same shot. But it's not exactly legal. Players often grant these to each other in recreational play to make the game more enjoyable. A mulligan allows golfers to revise their stance, grip, club selection, swing, or mindset, resulting in what they hope will be a better shot, and consequently, a better (albeit somewhat inaccurate) score.

In life, we don't get do-overs; but we do get revisions. We can re-see and re-do things as we learn and grow.

We can revise, or change, our perspective, our attitude, our careers, and our choices. It is the same with writing. Perhaps we can present revision to our students, in writing and in life, as a way of simply re-seeing and re-thinking—and a chance at re-doing. It doesn't mean they failed the first time, but that they have the power to imagine things differently, look at other possibilities, enlarge perceptions, and allow alternatives. It might be exciting for students to think about reinventing themselves and their writing, and learn to embrace revision as a blessing and not a curse.

There are a few different strategies I use to encourage revision. I have learned to have students email me their drafts. I have a disease that plagues many English teachers; if a student hands me a paper to look at, I pick up a pencil. This becomes editing. I am unable to allow mistakes to exist on a page. However, if the student emails me the paper I find I am better able to email comments back to the student without doing things for him. I may say, "You lack a clear thesis in your intro, although your lead is quite catchy." Or: "Your first body paragraph has good examples to support your points, but after that you lack depth and examples for each subsequent point." Or "Strengthen your transitions between points and paragraphs." This makes the student's second look at his paper about *revising*, not editing, which will occur much later in the process.

I also like this for the insight it gives me into student learning. For example, if I see in the emailed draft that a student has a clear run-on problem, instead of writing "run-ons" on a paper and leaving it up to him to either figure out how to correct them or get someone else to correct them, or neither, I can email him: "You have a run-on problem throughout the paper. Stop by my office after school or at lunch and we can clear it up in five minutes." Indeed, that's about how long it takes one-on-one to show students why they have run-ons and how to easily correct them. Email is an easy way to force students into the revision process prior to giving them editing feedback.

We have all experienced trying to get students to help their peers. The "swap papers" method results in editing. If I put a paper on the overhead, students want to point out every spelling or grammatical error (which for some reason they can see on others' papers but not their own) instead of commenting on the content of the writing. To combat this I often use a revision activity, or "game," called **Fishbowl.**

Students have been working on essays and are prepared to turn in their final drafts. (If you tell them it's a rough or early draft you will get poor quality or incomplete papers, so trick them. Go ahead. It's allowed.) Stop them by saying, "Wait. Before you turn those assignments in, let's play Fishbowl." One student volunteers to be in the Fishbowl and read her paper aloud to the class. Each of the other students divides a piece of paper into two columns. On the left side they may want to put a smiley face, a check, a plus sign—anything that indicates this is the strong side. Here they will list three things they hear that are done well, or that they like about the paper. On the right side of the paper they will put a minus sign, a question mark, or a sad face. In this column they will list the things they hear in the essay that can be improved. I tell students to try for three things in each column. They write these while the student is reading, and for a couple of minutes after she finishes. Then students share these comments with the reader. If a student says something that others have also written down, I tell them to lift their hands; this lets the author evaluate the comment accordingly.

Teachers may want to put a word wall up for students of the academic language and things they can be listening for, such as thesis, vocabulary, diction, organization, clarity, voice, transitions, support, etc. until they become expert critics. We do this once or twice as a whole group and then break into smaller groups to allow more students to be in the Fishbowl. Students who do not read their papers this time are first the next time. All students then get to take their papers and revise them before submitting the actual final draft.

Teachers may allow struggling learners or shy students to participate in this activity one-on-one, but they still need to read their papers aloud and make and share their lists. The key is not to let students just swap papers, or put them on the overhead, because then it becomes about editing. They need to read them aloud. The goal is to have students talking about their writing, using the vocabulary of writing, and the big ideas and decisions during the process. This will help them answer assessment questions about revision, which feature academic vocabulary, and also substantially improve their own writing.

Another way to encourage students to think and talk about the writing process is to keep the topic the same but change the purpose, such as from expository to persuasive. I may change the audience, from social media to your mother (for my senior high students); or the length of the essay. Condensing is a good skill for students to learn in an age where everything they fill out online has text boxes or word limits. This type of revision teaches them to be concise but precise in their decisions as writers.

Another way to improve revision habits in students is to assess their ability to use online writing tools, such as copy, cut, paste, bold, and italics. We tend to take for granted that our students know everything there is to know about computers, but most of what they know and do, such as web page design, social media, and gaming, is Internet related. They have less word processing skills now even than they used to. If we want them to revise, we must be sure they know how; we must teach them to use the tools available during the online revising and editing processes.

An area that has changed in both process and product is teaching research. We have all noticed by now that the card catalog is gone. The note cards with bibliographic information on them are gone. The books outlining MLA form: RIP. But the skills of research will always be relevant: knowing where, and how, to find information; knowing what is credible and what is not; understanding what is legal and what is not; knowing how to synthesize information to reach a conclusion, perform a task or learn something new. These skills are valuable and must be taught.

Many teachers believe that because they allow some Internet sources, they have "modernized" the research paper. For years, though, I kept the library component: I allowed a certain number of Internet or online data base sources, but still required the trip to the library to pore over dusty, yellowed, hard bound critical analysis treatises from Ze Olt Masters on Shakespeare, Twain, Hemingway, alcohol abuse, or the death penalty. I was the poster child for Prensky's quip: "Anyone who maintains that we should continue to teach and use both the old ways and the new is suggesting that we maintain an expensive horse in the barn in case our car breaks down." (2013). In my classroom, we used a car, so I felt good about my progress in keeping up with the modern world, but we also used a horse, because I had used a horse. I knew how to use a horse. I was comfortable assessing a horse.

Not only are the new voices not in many of the hard copy sources in libraries, but by the very nature of this kind of research, kids aren't interested. It becomes a school skill, not a life skill; they believe they will never use it or do it again in their lives. It reinforces that the classroom has nothing to do with life outside of school, and that I am old-fashioned (or just old) and a tyrant. Incidentally, the word "library" today no longer conjures up images of old volumes of books, but instead computers, work stations, I-Pads, and Kindles. Today's librarian has reinvented herself into a newer, sexier technology genius that young people enjoy asking for help. We must follow her lead.

Teachers can let students know that online databases and Internet sources are available, but so are books; and let *them* decide how best to research for their own purposes. Give them ownership of their learning. Whether the goal is to argue responsibly and passionately for a cause or examine the archetypes in Poe, that and the students' own learning styles and personalities should determine which sources they will use and where they will find them. We must hang on to the value: teaching our students to locate and evaluate research, synthesize information, and express opinions articulately and passionately. But we must encourage engagement and embrace ingenuity and diversity. Teach them the values and skills, but with the content and resources (and ease and speed) they have available to them.

Many teachers are often even more reluctant to change the student product and method of assessment than the packaging, delivery, or process. We allow I-Pad searches, unlimited Internet sources, and even the use of the Cloud or Drop Box to store research materials. We teach and allow the use of online citation guides and automatic citation generators, though somewhat grudgingly, because after all, *we* had to memorize where every single comma and period went and one misstep meant points deducted! But we hold on to that research paper. We want this many pages, typed, double spaced, MLA form, with a Works Cited page.

What is the likelihood that our students will produce that again in their careers? The product must also be changed, made relevant to today's purposes, audiences, topics, and genres. Perhaps an interactive Power Point or other multi-media presentation with embedded research, sound, video, links, photos, graphs, and interviews, that presents research and information or sways opinions, would be more appropriate, entertaining and powerful for audiences today. I know, I know: we wrote twelve page documented research papers. But we didn't have Animoto, Powtoons, or YouTube.

There are just so many options for engaging products. Instead of writing the traditional research paper, one alternative assignment with which I have found success is "The Outstanding Person of the Last 100 Years." Students express their interests for careers and hobbies and we list all these on the board. They then write their first two choices or primary interests on a card, and have to group themselves with others who share the same interests or career goals. Each group then researches three people who have greatly impacted their chosen field in the last 100 years, and prepares a multi-media persuasive presentation to convince the class who is the most outstanding. The project is accompanied by a one page written persuasive document, which includes short paragraphs, bulleted lists or hyperlinks, a separate works cited page, and in-text citations.

Students are required to use primary sources in the presentations—so we are treated to action clips and interviews of LeBron James and Willy Mayes (Outstanding Athlete nominees); various scenes from outstanding Broadway producers' work; or the inspiring or heartbreaking speeches of Presidents and leaders in foreign affairs. Last year we watched clips of education gurus Sir Ken Robinson and Dr. Robert Marzano, were treated to quotes and the "big ideas" from their latest works, and discussed the impact each had on education before the class voted Robinson the Outstanding Educator of the Last 100 Years. (They were impressed by his passion about creativity.)

We saw horrifying interviews with serial killers and their victims' loved ones as the class had to decide which serial killer had the most impact on law enforcement. Students stood at stations with computers as future computer scientists demonstrated what people would not be able to do, most of which we do every day, without the outstanding contributors in their field. After each presentation the class voted a winner in each category, and each group then went back to work to prepare to convince the class that the winner in their field should be the winner overall, the most Outstanding Person of the Last 100 Years.

Through this activity, I taught my students the essential curricular components of media, persuasive writing, research, revision, editing, and oral presentation. These presentations were not unlike those they may make in their careers. And they loved it. We had so much fun. There is no way I would have gotten such high quality of work from them in the last four weeks of school, in a five page documented critical analysis paper on poetry. I changed the content, but kept the skills and values intact.

Another topic students have researched for me is the one change people could make that would have the most important impact on the environment, or humanity in general. Ideas include getting rid of plastic water bottles, plastic bags, or cars that emit gases; planting rainforests and reviving natural habitats; requiring buses, bikes, or car pools; and more. Students produce commercials advertising the change and research that shows exactly the causes and effects of the action or product on the environment; then they participate in discussions and decide which change would be most effective. These types of multi-media products engage students and allow them to connect class work to their real lives, and possibly make a real difference, as was the case with one struggling student in another teacher's 9th grade ELA class.

Students were asked to choose a cause close to home and create a persuasive media presentation urging people to act. Tori chose for her persuasive writing task to create a commercial for "Dress for a Cure," asking girls to donate prom dresses for resale, the proceeds of which would go to a beloved local cancer victim. Using Animoto, an online multi-media writing tool, she added music and photos to concise and powerful text. She cited the cost of chemotherapy, the waste of most expensive prom dresses that sit in closets, and the opportunity to make a difference for not only the cancer patients but for girls who cannot afford to buy brand new dresses. She raised awareness and raised money as a result of this video she made for class, and she raised her own self-esteem and confidence as well.

Even shorter, daily assessments can take on a new look. My 11th grade students read *The Secret Life of Bees*. It is absolutely delightful to actually be able to watch clips on the definitive moments of the time period alluded to in the novel. Students are intrigued as they watch LBJ sign the Civil Rights Act, or see American Bandstand in its glory days. We watch The Supremes and Miles Davis perform; we see old signs advocating or protesting "Dixie," "Goldwater for President," and the Vietnam War. There are about fifty references to events of the time and students split them up, research them, and present them quickly and enjoyably for the class. This is a good pair with the short critical writing assignment I mentioned earlier in the chapter: they can view all these references; and then write which three they feel are most definitive of the time period.

If we teach the fundamentals of writing, the grammar and building blocks of structure and style; show students how to make choices and organize during the pre-writing process; require social interaction and revision during the writing process; allow alternative and current methods and products; and use our classroom reading to teach writing; we can teach more students to write passionately, fluently, effectively, and articulately. We will teach more students to write correctly. It is not easy, but it can be done, and it is worth it.

Notes and Reflection

CHAPTER FIVE

A PLACE FOR GRACE

"A teacher asked Paul
what he would remember
from third grade, and he sat
a long time before writing
'this year sumbody tutched me
on the sholder'
and turned his paper in."

—excerpt from "Rain" by Naomi Shihab Nye,
WORDS UNDER THE WORDS

CHAPTER 5

A PLACE FOR GRACE

-Johann Wolfgang von Goethe said "Treat a man as he is and he will remain as he is. Treat a man as he can and should be and he will become as he can and should be." This is the essence of grace. Grace is giving someone what he doesn't deserve. It is seeing beyond what someone is to what he can be. It is the greatest gift we can give our students. It is the precursor to second chances and third chances and the reason people eventually succeed. There is a parable in the Bible known as the Parable of the Prodigal Son, reprinted here from Luke 15:11-32 (NIV).

[11] Jesus continued: "There was a man who had two sons. [12] The younger one said to his father, 'Father, give me my share of the estate.' So he divided his property between them.

[13] "Not long after that, the younger son got together all he had, set off for a distant country and there squandered his wealth in wild living. [14] After he had spent everything, there was a severe famine in that whole country, and he began to be in need. [15] So he went and hired himself out to a citizen of that country, who sent him to his fields to feed pigs. [16] He longed to fill his stomach with the pods that the pigs were eating, but no one gave him anything.

[17] "When he came to his senses, he said, 'How many of my father's hired servants have food to spare, and here I am starving to death! [18]

I will set out and go back to my father and say to him: Father, I have sinned against heaven and against you. [19] I am no longer worthy to be called your son; make me like one of your hired servants.' [20] So he got up and went to his father.

"But while he was still a long way off, his father saw him and was filled with compassion for him; he ran to his son, threw his arms around him and kissed him.

"The son said to him, 'Father, I have sinned against heaven and against you. I am no longer worthy to be called your son.'

"But the father said to his servants, 'Quick! Bring the best robe and put it on him. Put a ring on his finger and sandals on his feet. [23] Bring the fattened calf and kill it. Let's have a feast and celebrate. [24] For this son of mine was dead and is alive again; he was lost and is found.' So they began to celebrate.

"Meanwhile, the older son was in the field. When he came near the house, he heard music and dancing. [26] So he called one of the servants and asked him what was going on. [27] 'Your brother has come,' he replied, 'and your father has killed the fattened calf because he has him back safe and sound.'

[28] "The older brother became angry and refused to go in. So his father went out and pleaded with him. [29] But he answered his father, 'Look! All these years I've been slaving for you and never disobeyed your orders. Yet you never gave me even a young goat so I could celebrate with my friends. [30] But when this son of yours who has squandered your property with prostitutes comes home, you kill the fattened calf for him!'

[31] "'My son,' the father said, 'you are always with me, and everything I have is yours. [32] But we have to celebrate and be glad, because this brother of yours was dead and is alive again; he was lost and is found.'"

In this story, the younger son asks for, receives, and squanders away his portion of his inheritance from his father. In asking, he greatly offended his father and culture, more or less wishing his father was dead. In receiving, he must have caused his father to sell property, cash in assets, and disgrace himself publicly. In squandering, he committed a multitude of sins and embarrassed his family. Upon realization that he had nothing left and was starving, the prodigal son travels back to his father's estate, intending to just feed and eat with his father's pigs. But the father sees him coming, far away, and *runs* to meet him. He *runs* to meet him. The father, an older man, holds up his tunic, crying, "My son," and runs to meet him. The father tells the servants: "Kill the best calf! We're having a party! My son, my son is home!"

The son deserves ignominy, disgrace, punishment. At the very least, he deserves the "I told you so" speech. But the father instead offers grace.

This is not all there is to the story. The older brother is not so quick to forgive. The older brother played by the rules. He stayed home, he worked hard, took care of aging parents, did not drink too much or chase women. The older brother is outraged. We are killing the best cow for him? What about me? I've been here all along, and we eat hot dogs! Sandwiches! He doesn't deserve this kind of welcome, this kind of party. The older brother did not understand grace. Nor did I for many years, and it limited my relationships with family members and students alike.

I operated my life and my classroom more on a system of justice. I was firm and fair, but fairness to me meant equality; it meant everyone had to meet *my* expectations and do things *my* way, on my terms and my time table.

There were consequences for actions. Few second chances, no mulligans. I expected people to do right. I protected myself from those that didn't. I loved, and taught, the kids that were easy to love, and teach.

I now understand that Grace runs to meet *all* the students, regardless of where they are coming from, what they've done, or how many times they've disappointed me. Grace re-teaches with the same enthusiasm. Grace is unwilling to punish a child for his parents' working late and his being left alone; or his having no parents; or his having parents in jail or on drugs. But it is important to realize that grace goes one step further: it means not punishing the child—too much—or holding a grudge, for his *own* bad choices, for his own decision to play ball or go to a party instead of writing the essay or reading the article. Grace recognizes but does not condemn human frailty, fallibility, or flaws. Grace offers concern, gentle correction, and consistent love—not condemnation. With grace we are indeed able to see beyond what a student is to what he can be, and *treat him as if he already were.*

If we are going to err in education, in administering punishments or assigning grades, I would rather err on the side of grace. I have learned this in part through having a brother who is an alcoholic. I wasted a lot of years being mad at my brother. My sister and I called him the "prodigal son," because truly, my mother killed the fatted calf and ran to meet him every time he showed up sober. At some point, though, I realized several truths that changed how I treat my brother, and my students.

It occurred to me that I had a choice, to appreciate and enjoy the times he is present, and sober, and be kind to him; or be angry and resentful, and ruin the good times because of the bad. Likewise, I can enjoy my students, and appreciate when they are present, and have their homework, instead of holding a grudge because of repeated absences, or repeated failure to complete assignments. I can allow the time I do spend with them to be productive and not waste it resenting things I can't control.

I realized one day that my brother does not *want* to be an alcoholic; he does not *want* to disappoint people who love him. He isn't doing it to hurt *me*, specifically. My students, also, want to be successful, and included, and loved. They don't want to fail. I have had to learn not to take their failures or mistakes or behaviors personally. Surely, as I tell them, their lack of preparation is not my emergency. But as I tell myself, it isn't a personal affront, either. It was a great day when I realized that *I* could run to meet my brother, too. I am not responsible for what other people do, or don't do; but I am responsible for my own actions. I would rather they be guided by grace. I want to run to meet my students. While it is true that sometimes giving grace doesn't help a person in the way we want it to, withholding it doesn't, either. And with the former, you sleep better at night—perhaps because you are tired from all the running.

Mike (not his real name) was a student in my evening class at the local community college where I adjunct. He was sporadically genius. His attendance was intermittent; his attitude, unpredictable; his work, brilliant—when he did it. I did not see him. I saw a student who missed too many classes, who didn't care enough to turn in work when it was due, who didn't shower, and who was unkempt and disheveled. He was wasting away his potential while others who had none of his ability were struggling so much in the class to be successful. I suspected Mike had even come to class drunk a couple of times. Then one night, he didn't have his homework, he smelled of sweat and alcohol, looked horrible, and I had had enough. I asked him to stay after class. I was ready to unleash on him for missing two weeks straight. "I haven't been here," he stammered, "because I have been in jail and then detox."

And I looked at this young man, and I suddenly saw him. I saw how hard it must be *on him;* I saw that he did not want to be a failure, and certainly he did not want to be an alcoholic. I saw also my brother. And I know my brother is brilliant. It is an ongoing struggle for him, but he has a beautiful family and a good job and contributes and serves in education more than almost anyone I know. And I wonder how many times in his life people were at that crossroads with him, a place where they had to choose between grace and justice. And I am so thankful someone chose grace.

My brother has influenced me on many occasions as an educator. Chantel (also not her real name) was another adult student in my evening class. She could not write one grammatically correct sentence, but could clean up a drunk and hold him for two days while he shook violently, or was sick and cursing and lashing out. I knew this because most evenings she wore her work shirt to class, on which was the logo from a local rehabilitation facility that had recently housed my brother. "Yeah, I know him," she said when I asked her. Her eyes lit up with the passion I have when I talk about my students, and teaching. "He's a tough one because he's so smart. He tries to outsmart all of us, the system, even his own self. He ain't ready yet," she finished, shaking her head sadly. "That man gon need my help."

If she could show this grace and use her gifts to try and save my brother in this way, surely I could spend a little extra time after class to teach her how to use a comma. She was required to pass this course for any kind of promotion in her career, which would put her in a better position to reach and help more people, people like my brother. She was as good at her job as I try to be at mine. I saw Chantel suddenly through eyes of love. I saw her gifts, her kindness, and I loved, accepted, and respected her for who she was. I had infinitely more patience with her than I would have had just a year or two before, before I started allowing myself to see other people, and specifically my students, through the eyes of grace.

High school teachers have a plethora of duties in addition to teaching classes. We sponsor clubs, coach teams, and serve on committees. On one such committee, I had to sit on a board for an expulsion hearing for a student, accused (well, caught) of violating the substance abuse policy. Clearly, he *deserved* to be expelled from the club, and admitted as much; however, he requested a chance to plead with the committee for an alternate punishment. He admitted he had made a mistake. He asked for grace.

We allowed this student to remain in the club on probation, complete drug awareness courses and community service, and teach his peers the lessons he learned. I do not know that our decision was best. It was agonizing having to cast a vote to decide this sort of thing. It came down to this: expelling him from the club would definitely *not* change the behavior. It would serve as a warning to other students, certainly, to not get caught. But it wasn't going to change their values. When I coached, I used extrinsic punishment to change surface behaviors. Running lines or laps certainly deters tardiness, for example. However, my goal was not to have athletes be on time because they didn't want to run. It was to have them realize that being on time for things is a valued life skill that demonstrates respect, responsibility, and unselfishness. Extrinsic punishment must never replace intrinsic lessons.

I, and other committee members, in the case of the student in violation of the substance abuse policy, knew that justice would not change his behavior, and perhaps even have the opposite effect. But we hoped grace and kindness might at least give him pause and something to remember in the coming months and years. This is not to say that there are not consequences for actions. I tell my students all the time: we live in our consequences, daily. But the goal is to teach and have students learn. We must ask ourselves not only with instructional decisions but also with behavioral ones: What do we want them to learn and be able to do? And how best can we achieve this?

Answering these questions inspired the famous "lunch with Ms. Mayer." It's ironic that I have a reputation of being one of the hardest teachers in our district. It isn't for reasons one might think, though it started out that way some years ago. I am considered hard not because I will give zeroes for work that is not completed, but because *I won't*. I am hard because I expect that students will do what I ask them to do, successfully, no matter what it takes, and anything less is unacceptable.

For example, my students know that if they do not succeed on a writing assignment, or fail to complete it, they will have lunch with me the next day, and for as many days as it takes, until the work is acceptable. I tell them this is not punishment; it is opportunity. While elementary students might see this lunch with the teacher as a real treat, my high school students are *not* thrilled to have to remain on campus (we have open campus) and eat lunch in my classroom with me while completing assignments. They tell each other, "She won't let you just take the zero, dude; you might as well do it the first time." And it's true. But I explain to them, that this is grace.

It would be easier for them (and me) if I just assigned a zero and moved on. And, I'd get to eat my lunch in peace. But then there would be wailing and gnashing of teeth when grades are finalized. I might still be considered a hard teacher; but would I be considered an effective one? The student who gets up in the morning solely to run track or play basketball wouldn't get to run or play ("No pass, no play"). Somebody else wouldn't graduate because of immaturity or addiction or an unsupportive home life. Many students would never get a chance to see if maybe in a different setting with a little more time and instruction, they could in fact learn some writing skills that will be so necessary in their lives.

Grace says no excuses, and lots of opportunities. In my system, the students will feel good about their grades, and learning; I will feel good about myself; and they will be more inclined to just do it right the first time, next time. An added benefit of these lunches is the setting they provide in which to build relationships with reluctant or resistant students. Since our students are not always mature enough to make the decision to "do right," I extend to them grace, cleverly disguised as "lunch with Ms. Mayer."

In the fable "The Wind and the Sun" a man is walking with a coat wrapped tightly around him and the wind and the sun wager to see who can get the man to take off his coat. The more furiously the wind blows, the tighter the man wraps the coat around himself. But the sun shines gently, persistently, until the man is warm and removes the coat of his own will. The sun achieves the desired outcome, not with bluster and force, but with gentleness and opportunity. I have learned that while some students need the wind to motivate them (and this is differentiation, after all), most respond better to the sun.

Perhaps understanding grace and caring about my students' lives beyond the walls of my classroom is why I teach them what I call "life lessons." If I truly believe I teach people first, then skills, then content, I need to teach my students what they need to know to live fulfilling, productive, well-balanced lives outside the walls of my classroom. I need to help them grow into adults. These short life lessons, which I offer briefly to my 12th graders on Fridays during second semester, include such things as how the emotional bank account works. I teach my students that every day they are making withdrawals or deposits into other people, and the more deposits they make the more likely they are to be able to make a withdrawal when they need it. If they are always pleasant, have work in on time, and participate in class, then when they are having a bad day, the teacher is more apt to be understanding of their situation if they forgot to complete an assignment or are inadvertently rude or distracted. They will have credit in their account. If they constantly make withdrawals without ever making a deposit, pretty soon they come up empty. I teach them to make deposits early and often in their relationships with teachers, family, friends, and employers.

Another life lesson I teach students is to "set your mind before it's time." This involves deciding what they believe is right for them about things like experimenting with certain drugs or sex, or honesty with money, or cheating in school. Then they will already have made the decision *before* they are in the heat of moment with a hot babe, *before* someone hands them the illegal substance, *before* they find that the cashier has given them $100 too much change, and *before* a buddy asks to copy their test. It won't be an issue or internal debate right then when they may not be thinking clearly, because they will have already set their minds what they will do in that situation. A little forethought and preparation goes a long way.

I teach them the life lesson of having a philosophy of money, sharing with them mine: "Give some, save some, spend some." Along with this I show them how investing and borrowing work. I am amazed at how little they know about interest, and credit cards. They will get that first credit card when they go to college. Mine was a Diamond Shamrock card (I think this is Valero, now). This was gold to a broke nineteen year old college sophomore. I could now put more than $1.00 worth of gas in my car at a time. I soon realized Diamond Shamrock stocked bread and lunchmeat as well, and a whole host of other items I could certainly use, like cereal, milk, chips, soft drinks, and aspirin. Why, they even sold beer! Diamond Shamrock became my Walmart. I could make a day of it. Until that day I got the bill, and I realized: They were charging me for all that stuff! I called them, and tried to explain that I didn't have any money; I was a broke college student! There must be some mistake. Alas. The CEO of Diamond Shamrock apparently did not share my same philosophy of grace, and had not heard about any bail-out plan, either. But perhaps I can keep my students from making the same mistakes I made, if I just take time to share with them some little things they need to know about college and life besides reading and writing.

Offering grace to students is a life lesson in itself. Grace means allowing students to save face. Through grace I am able to recognize that student resistance is often due to larger issues. Maybe the student doesn't know how to ask for help. Maybe he or she is hurting—and it is a life lesson to recognize that hurt people, hurt people, and sometimes we have to let things go.

There are so many little things our students do not always learn at home that they need to know to be able to function as fully realized human beings in the world. I am an English Language Arts teacher, yes. But it only takes fifteen minutes a week to teach my students how to make good decisions, impress a job interviewer, understand and practice grit, or even properly set a table. Yet every year, when I ask them on the final exam to reflect on the most significant things they learned in English class, they always mention the life lessons as something they will never forget. I am reminded that I am teaching people, not content, and people need to learn things that they want to learn for their life purposes; and people need grace. I am reminded that my students may not remember all that I say, or that we do, in my classroom. But they will always remember how I made them feel. I want to be remembered as the sun and not the wind.

Many of us have seen Broadway adaptations of the French historical novel, *Les Miserables,* by Victor Hugo, which depicts the battle between grace and justice. In it Jean Valjean is released from prison after serving nineteen years for the crimes of stealing bread to feed his sister's starving children, and then attempting to escape. Upon his release he cannot find work because he is a convict, and must sleep on the street. When the Bishop takes him in for the night, the bitter Valjean promptly steals his silver. He is apprehended quickly and brought back to the Bishop, who exclaims to his angry and ashamed face: "Ah! Here you are. I am glad to see you. Well, but how is this? I *gave you* the candlesticks too, which are of silver like the rest, and for which you can certainly get two hundred francs. Why did you not carry them away with your forks and spoons?"

The Bishop instructs Valjean that he must use the silver—the grace—that was given to him to become a good man. Jean Valjean is thunderstruck in the face of such kindness, and he eventually does become the man the Bishop saw. He "pays it forward," and then some. He is pursued relentlessly for all of his life by justice, though, in the form of one merciless policeman, Javert, who cannot see past a man's transgressions to his transformation. In the end Valjean is at peace in death, as he has received and given grace and love throughout his life; while Javert, bitter, angry, and alone, never understands the concept and takes his own life.

This story poignantly portrays what love can do. And every time I see this play on Broadway, I am reminded again not only how long it is, because it is *one long play*, but also, that grace has the power to save more lives, and minds, than justice. The father in the story of the prodigal son did not remind his son of everything he did wrong. He just focused on the one thing his son did right: he came home. The son, and our students, and my brother, already know what they have done wrong. They have more than enough regret and remorse and don't need someone to make them feel worse. Probably they wouldn't respond to that very well anyway. In life and in the classroom, there's a reason why there is a "grace that is greater than all our sins." And all of us, at some point in our lives and careers, must choose to be Javert, or the Bishop, to our own Jean Valjean.

Notes and Reflection

CHAPTER SIX

FEEDBACK & GRADING

"Come to the edge. We might fall.

Come to the edge. It's too high.

Come to the edge. So they came

and he pushed and they flew."

—Christopher Logue

CHAPTER 6

FEEDBACK & GRADING

Broaching the controversial subject of grading in a faculty meeting is like bringing up religion or politics at dinner. It's taboo. And yet how can teachers still grade the same way when educational standards, rigor, assessments, technology, teacher evaluations, lesson design, and even psychology, have changed? If we are a standards-based system, and all of us are, then grades should measure and reflect our students' mastery of standards, *not the route they take to achieve mastery.* Many times our grades measure home life, support systems, medication taken, hours worked, behavior, motivation, addiction, attendance, maturity, timeliness, responsibility, or speed. "But if our mission is to teach so that all students learn, we cannot let their immaturity dictate their destiny." (Wormeli, 2011) I believe all teachers must consider from time to time what we really believe about grading. What is the real purpose of grades in school?

Recent retest laws have some teachers up in arms. The law requires that a student be offered a re-test if he or she did not pass the first test. Some teachers refuse outright, saying the student had ample time to study and should have been prepared for the first test. Their thinking is that it was, after all, on the syllabus. If the project was due on Monday, and this student didn't have it, it isn't fair to the other students to accept it late. If a student makes a 40 on a test, it's not fair to the one who studied and made an 85 to give the student who didn't adequately prepare a re-test. If Rob's essay scored 90 and was turned in on time, and it took John three extra days, he should not receive the same grade no matter how good the work is, because he missed the deadline. This is how I felt for a long time.

Like many teachers, I was the kid in school who made the 90 the first time and never missed a deadline. I remember as a young student being frustrated that those who didn't "do right" were given another chance, when I sometimes had to work very hard to get it right and on time, but still did it. Teenagers, after all, don't realize that injustice on the surface is just a drop in the bucket; I now know how blessed I was, and how the injustices to children that show up in grades and inability to meet deadlines are indeed as deep as the ocean.

Accountability and hard work are certainly to be stressed and praised. But lawyers can take the bar more than once, and their law degree does not distinguish this. Pilot's license tests, auto mechanic certification exams, and SAT tests can all be redone. Teachers may not pass the exit test the first time they take it, to teach science, or government, or music, or even English Language Arts. To say I am preparing students for the real world by not allowing a re-test is a fallacy. The real world allows different paces, second chances, and occasional do-overs, which all yield the same result. I certainly did not learn how to use technology in my classroom at the same pace as some of my colleagues. I have learned it is better for my students and me to achieve mastery later, rather than never because of an irrevocably missed deadline.

Another thing I have learned about grading is that averaging grades does not make sense, particularly in a standards based system. For example, if a student makes a 40 on an assignment the second week of the grading period, and I provide feedback and the student learns and improves and takes another test the 4th week of the grading period, where knowledge on the same material is essential, and he scores an 80, why would I say the student has earned a 60, or has mastered 60% of the standards? Clearly, he mastered 80% of the standards, just not at the same time as a classmate.

Runners can lose twenty races before setting the world record. All those previous times aren't averaged. While it is true that an Olympic runner does not get a do-over if he performs poorly during the big race, he is in the proficient runner stage, not the learning-to-run stage. Can you imagine telling a runner that his earlier 60.74 seconds from two months ago would be averaged with his new and improved 51.03 seconds, and that he would be assessed on an average of his failures and successes? We evaluate only the *improved* performance of artists and athletes and many professionals; only in school do we average where people used to be with where they are now (Wormeli, 2011).

It could be that the student who received an 80 the first time *already knew the standards measured* when he or she came to my class. For example, if I give my students a list of twenty vocabulary words, it is likely that more advanced students in the class, and students who read, will already know half of the words. So these students are more likely to score 80 on a quiz, since to get an 80 they really only have to learn six new words. The quiz grades then are not a measure of how effective my teaching strategies are or aren't, or how much the students study, but rather, a test of students' prior knowledge. If, by the fifth week of the grading period, we have used the words and made them part of students' working vocabularies, so that when I test again, the student who scored 40 now scores 90, suggesting he has mastered 90% of the words, why would I average these grades?

If we do not allow retests or second attempts, and we average grades, *what then is the point of instruction?* We are telling students, no matter how well you learn the material after the test date, you can't change the grade. I am all for holding students accountable—for l*earning*, not for past mistakes or for what they knew when they started in my class. They will be more apt to be accountable for their own learning, and desire to continue to learn, when there is an opportunity to demonstrate it in a setting that matters to them. One such setting is grade improvement.

Imagine telling a student: I still want you to learn this, because it's an important skill, so come to tutorials, but even if you learn it, the grade remains an F. What is the motivation for students to put forth any effort? At such young ages they may not be intrinsically motivated, or committed to constant self-improvement. Furthermore, they may not care about our content or the skills we teach (shocking, I know). It is hard to inspire continued improvement for which there is no manifested reward or acknowledgment.

When my 12th grade students turned in their personal narratives early this year, it was quickly apparent that more than 60% of them regularly wrote run-on sentences, and had no idea they were doing it. They also had a tendency to "tell" instead of "show" the reader the details and descriptions in the narratives. I graded these papers according to my rubric, requirements, and standards for this grade level and this assignment. But on the day I returned them, we revisited some professional and mentor texts and reviewed some of the traits of good narrative writing. I reminded students how to use dialogue to convey details and make scenes come to life. I also gave a grammar lesson. I showed students why correct sentence structure and punctuation are important, and then how to avoid run-ons by using semi-colons, conjunctions, and periods. Finally, I told students they had to take my suggestions for both revising and editing, and rewrite the narratives and re-submit them to me by the end of the week, and I would re-grade them. Not average the grades—re-grade them.

Two things make this activity successful: First, it isn't optional. Though some students are thrilled to be allowed to work on their narratives and resubmit them, there are students who would be just fine with a 70, or who don't care enough about grades to re-do it even if they fail. Then learning would not take place. So, I require these rewrites. I even provide them a setting: lunch with Ms. Mayer. Also, the grade will be changed to reflect the new demonstrated mastery level. Students have to believe there is a reason for doing this work. The point of instruction is to take students from where they are to where they can be, to the best they can be. Grades should reflect their (and my) best effort.

Often we as teachers subconsciously believe we are supposed to have a certain number of A's, or B's, or F's. But year to year classes vary. In a standards based system, students should be scored against mastery of the standard, not each other. If all students perform miserably on a test or assignment, a B should not indicate who performed "less miserably." (Guskey, 2011) We should not be grading for ranking purposes, though this is what happens. I have had teachers tell me many times over the years that if they grade a certain class, such as 10th grade English, in this particular year like they usually do no one will pass, or no one will receive an A, because the class overall is just weak. Or they grade an unusually strong class against each other so they won't have too many A's. Teachers feel an unspoken pressure not to have too many students get low grades, or high grades. So we may unintentionally *adjust the standards* to account for differences in student performances, so we will still have the "right" amount of A's, B's, C's, D's, and F's.

That pressure we feel though should be more about how to differentiate instruction so all students are able to master the standards as they are. "To succeed with standards-based grading, teachers need to develop teaching and learning strategies, formative assessment strategies, and coaching strategies at least as much as they need to develop grading plans. They need to develop skill at differentiating instructional avenues to the standards so that most students can reach them." (Brookhart, 2011)

Without intervention, certainly, there are classes where grades will resemble a bell-shaped curve; and classes where a large percentage of students will fall on the low end, or the high end, of a curve. But teaching is intervention! (Guskey, 2011) Part of teaching is knowing what students need to learn, assessing where they are, and actively implementing a plan to enable them to master, and in many cases go beyond, the standards with success. I have learned that it is not a badge of honor to have students fail my class. It is honorable to keep the expectations at and beyond the standard, and have them succeed.

One purpose grades serve is to inform instruction. Grades let teachers know if they are presenting effective instruction, and if students are indeed mastering the standards appropriate to their grade level. Grades also let students know how they are doing. However, that is not specific enough. To really aid instruction and cause learning, all assessment should be accompanied by feedback. I did not realize the value of feedback when I first began teaching. I now understand that giving feedback to students is more valuable than lecture, or grades, to cause learning. And it's a two-way street; feedback *from my students* can inform my instruction better than assessments can. Grades alone let students—and me—know *how* they are doing. Feedback tells us both *why*.

First, student feedback, if genuinely solicited in a safe environment, can inform instruction. I am finally humble enough to realize that sometimes when grades are poor, it's because *I* have something to learn. I have discovered it is not a weakness to ask students what they perceive my own weaknesses are, or how I can improve instruction for them. I used to assume when a student struggled in my class it was because of something *he or she* was or wasn't doing. It never occurred to me that there might be something *I* could change, however small, that would enable my students to succeed. I thought it was primarily up to the students to make the adjustments. I now believe when students struggle the first thing a teacher can do is ask: "What can I do to help you?"

I learned this by accident, from a struggling student, whom I will call Nate, in a conference. I often distribute a short reading assignment during class, give students a few minutes to read it, and then we discuss it. As a very slow reader, Nate said he always felt embarrassed that he was not finished reading when we started talking about the material, and he was unable to finish while we were talking, and so was unprepared to offer comments or contribute. And then, he said, he often never went back and finished it, even if it was interesting, because, "what was the point then, really?" He said if I would just give him the reading assignments a day prior to class, he would be glad to read them before class.

This was one of those moments as a teacher you just smack your own head and wonder: What was I thinking?

Indeed, how easy it is to give a week's worth of reading or more ahead of time, on a syllabus, website, or even paper copies, to students, with the understanding that should they wish to prepare in advance for the class, or want to get ahead, they can read them. Since I teach summary skills, the summary and notes they take while engaged in this prior reading would be adequate review for these students while others quickly read the material in class in preparation for discussion. This was not an isolated incident, but rather, one in a series of unrelated occurrences in a week's time that slammed home to me the importance of getting feedback from my students.

My students sit at tables in small groups, about three or four per table, and I randomly switch the groups every three weeks by shuffling cards with names on them and reseating students accordingly. I have learned that students need to share and receive opinions and responses with all students in the class, regardless of their social group or ability level. This truly has helped my students stay on task and have great discussions, and often make new, somewhat unlikely, friends or study partners. After one such re-grouping, the classroom atmosphere was unusually tense. In fact for three days we were unable to get much done: little participation, zero discussion, and furtive glances around the room. I had no idea why everything was falling flat and my students were so pre-occupied.

I passed out a feedback sheet on which I asked what I could do to improve the quality of instruction and help students both enjoy and benefit from the unit we were studying. Almost all students reported that Student A had betrayed Student B by cheating on her with her longtime boyfriend, and though they used to be close friends, no one could believe I had seated them together right after this. The students who were not involved, but aware, were so nervous waiting for the explosion, they could not concentrate on anything else. I lost three days not knowing this! There are those who say kids just have to learn to deal with things. Perhaps. But I think this would be hurtful, even to me, and I would not be in my best learning environment seated next to my ex-friend. I rearranged the seating chart and we made up for the lost days quickly.

One last example: Laurie (not her real name) repeatedly failed reading quizzes. She was a good writer, and an absolute pleasure in class, but every time I assigned reading in informational texts, she failed the quiz. I wrongly assumed she wasn't reading. Finally, she told me she was reading the material multiple times, but had no idea what was important, and couldn't remember anything she read. She had no idea how to approach the material, and was taking notes on almost every word of text so she wouldn't miss something important. I quickly realized that if Laurie was deficient in this area, many other students probably were also. We revisited our approach to reading informational texts, step by step. We practiced with shorter texts, and I modeled the strategies of preview, active recall, paraphrase, and summarize throughout the reading. This helped all my students and grades improved.

When I asked for feedback on a recent reading quiz, another student wrote that he often used the skills I had taught him to write a brief reflection or summary after reading. He wondered why he was doing that if I wasn't going to let him use it, or at least review it, prior to bombarding him with questions, quizzes, or more notes. He was right. If we review our material, and settle and focus our minds for a couple of minutes prior to starting anything, we are all more ready to receive instruction and demonstrate learning. Ask your students for feedback, and really listen. It is amazing what you will learn about their habits, skills, literacy experiences, and lives, which will enable and empower you to more effectively teach, and the students, to really learn.

Providing individual, specific, actionable feedback to students is perhaps the greatest instructional strategy there is. As a long time basketball player and coach, I like to consider myself a coach in the classroom as well. The word coach implies more interactive, individual, hands-on instruction—in other words, more feedback. John Maxwell writes,

> I read in my friend Kevin Hall's book *Aspire* that the word coach derives from the horse-drawn coaches

that were developed in the town of Kocs during the fifteenth century. The vehicles were originally used to transport royalty, but in time they also carried valuables, mail, and common passengers. As Kevin remarks, 'A coach remains something, or someone, who carries a valued person from where they are to where they want to be.' (2012)

Coaches rely on providing feedback to athletes to improve performance. The feedback is specific, immediate, and goal-oriented. When I coached, I expected my athletes to listen and apply feedback and improve their performance regardless of their skill level. The same is true in the classroom.

What constitutes feedback and how do we effectively provide it to students? "Feedback is actionable information, and it empowers the student to make intelligent adjustments." (Rapp, 2012) We have to tell each student something specific he or she can do differently to achieve a higher level of success. Praise and criticism are not feedback, because feedback refers to or is accompanied by instruction, and is actionable. A student can't act on "weak paragraph," specifically. "This paragraph lacks the depth of having several solid examples, which your others do," is feedback. "This introduction is good because it clearly sets forth a thesis and gives readers a reason to want to read more," is feedback. "Nice introduction" is not.

Feedback in a tutorial could be showing a student how to correct run-on sentences, but it is not editing a paper for the student, which would give the student a higher score but would not cause learning. Writing "too many run-ons" on the paper with a grade of "F" requires no action on the part of the student, and results only in resignation, not learning. Withholding the grade and writing "see me to address your run-on problem so you can re-submit" encourages learning on the part of the student. A student who follows up by coming to tutorials receives actionable feedback. He then will be able to correct his own run-ons and avoid them in the future, resulting in real learning, better grades, and better writing. We've all heard the proverb: "Give a man a fish, he eats for a day; teach him to fish, he eats for life." Give a student praise, or edit his paper, or criticize it with a grade and no follow-up, and there is no continuum of learning. Feedback causes real learning to occur, which "feeds" him for life.

For feedback to be actionable, students must use it immediately, while they are still working in that learning goal or objective (Rapp). Far too often, ELA teachers make the same black hole error as state-wide assessments, where students *never* receive specific feedback, only a score. Essays are returned and feedback given *after* the writing task or skill has been abandoned for something else. Sometimes papers are returned at the end of class and students cram them into backpacks and never even read the notes and comments suggesting how they might improve, much less apply them to something meaningful. Feedback should be given when it matters, while students can use it.

For example, on a recent multi-media presentation project my 11th grade students did not do a very good job. I gave each group and the entire class temporary grades and actionable feedback. I showed them specifically where they could integrate sources smoothly into the presentation; suggested ways to actively involve their audience; cautioned them not to read material on a power point aloud to the class; pointed out illegible or grammatically incorrect text; and suggested the use of links to some of their primary sources, interviews, or clips, to show the class rather than just list facts and sources. I had initially given them these guidelines on a rubric but apparently, as is so often the case, it wasn't enough. As I addressed each presentation I felt like they were able to see clearly how they could improve, and I could sense their eagerness to do so.

I ensured feedback would be tied to learning in two ways: I required them to go immediately and re-make the presentations, and I replaced the temporary grade with the grade they earned after learning had taken place. Then I gave a similar follow-up assignment a few weeks later, reminding them to use the feedback they received on the first round of projects. If students do poorly prior to feedback, perhaps my instruction was not explicit enough, or the assignment goals could be more effectively taught through individual feedback than whole class instruction. It is noteworthy that with feedback, students improved the performance greatly; this indicated to me there was a willingness to learn and to do well, but an initial disconnect, or lack of knowledge and skills. I cannot bemoan their ignorance; my paycheck depends on it, after all.

One way teachers can use specific feedback to cause learning is the rubric. The rubric takes the guesswork out of student assignments, provides transparency, and allows students to self-assess. It provides teachers a clear route to grading standards.

> Though the system as a whole is ultimately subjective—as I think any grading system must be—the rubric provides a small measure of objectivity by insisting that the teacher have a basis for the final assessment. Few things are more frustrating for students than unexplained grades ('Why is mine a 73 and hers a 78?'), and it is one of the great powers of the rubric to bring us closer to explaining the inherently inexplicable notion of what makes a piece of writing work. (Livingston, 2012)

The rubric gives me more confidence in my own grading, and, far more importantly, it gives students more confidence in the reliability of how they are being assessed. This in turn gives them confidence that they can improve their scores; they are not solely dependent on the whim of the grader, which they often believe.

"Comparing paper to paper, they can even begin to self-identify trends in need of strong correction. As previously stated, it is my experience that in practice this process of 'legitimizing' the final grade has the odd and positive effect of minimizing it: the students become more concerned about how they can craft a better argument, for instance, than in how they can get the elusive final 'A' mark on the paper as a whole." (Livingston, 2012) A rubric allows students to see the core problem or problems in a paper; thus, it serves as feedback not only for that specific assignment, but for future ones, for which it should inform their preparation and self-assessment.

Grades are a visual and numerical assessment of learning. They inform students where they are on the continuum that is mastery of specific standards. Grades are not supposed to represent an average of where they were last week or last month; or rank students against each other; or measure the route the students take to achieve mastery. There may be a margin of error in grading, because we are not perfect in our instruction or our assessment. Feedback causes learning, which propels students up the ladder of mastery. Feedback informs students *how* they can get to where they need to be, to the next level on the continuum. Grading and feedback should exist simultaneously.

TV evangelist Joyce Meyer likes to say, "I'm not where I need to be, but thank God I'm not where I used to be." This alludes to a work in progress, and has a tone of possibility rather than finality. So do grades, when accompanied by feedback and instruction. My most important duty in my job description is in the word itself: **teach**er. I am not called a "grader." Grades represent just one component of my classroom duties, and like any sub-category, they should serve to support the bigger idea. When linked with feedback, they do.

Notes and Reflection

CHAPTER SEVEN

THE POWER OF REFLECTION

"Facts are stupid things until brought into

connection with some general law."

—Samuel Scudder

CHAPTER 7

THE POWER OF REFLECTION

Closely tied to feedback is reflection, which is like feedback you immediately give yourself. To reflect is to constantly assess where you are and where you are going, and how you are doing in accomplishing what you want to accomplish. "It does little good to see something new without taking time to think about it. It does no good to hear something new without applying it. I've found that the best way to learn something new is to take time at the end of the day to ask yourself questions that prompt you to think about what you learned. "(Maxwell, 2012) It is imperative that teachers self-assess after every lesson, every class, every day, every year. When we reflect we think about why things went well, or poorly; we decide what to change, what to remember, and what to cherish. It is equally important that we insist our students regularly reflect on their learning.

We learn best when we process information for our own purposes. In his presentation at the Texas Council of Teachers of English Language Arts Annual Convention (January 2013), Jeff Anderson cited brain research showing that the only way we become really conscious of what is happening around us is to have a conversation about it. Whether it's discussing a movie with friends, or a staff development meeting with other teachers, the things we talk about and apply to our own situations, personalities, and experiences are the things we retain. Years later we will not remember everything about that movie or conference we attended, but we will remember the parts we discussed.

We need to make time to just think; to actively, purposely reflect on new learning and have a conversation about it. We need to do this after attending training sessions or conferences, after reading articles in our field or on education in general, and after meetings with colleagues. In my own presentations for teachers, I constantly have them stop and think about the concepts and strategies I suggest, and discuss how they can be applied in their own classrooms, for their own purposes. Otherwise activities are just nice to do, perhaps thought-provoking, but not life-changing. Learning is life-changing when it influences our actions. We must reflect at the end of every day on the choices we make for our students, classes, and lessons, and on our overall "performance": what went well, and what fell flat. Socrates said, "The unexamined life is not worth living." The unexamined day in the life of the teacher causes him or her to stagnate, to miss opportunities and blessings. Likewise our students must think about and talk about their learning throughout the school day.

Our classes are not set up to allow students to process new information. They go to a history class, and learn for 45 minutes; then the bell rings and they go to an English class. They participate in a lesson for 45 minutes; then the bell rings, and they go to a math class. I just wonder when students have time to reflect on what they have learned, make real life connections and practical applications, and just sit and think. We humans have begun to think of our lives like video games. If we make a colossal error, we just hit restart and begin again. We don't think about what caused the error, why we got blown up, or why we went down the wrong path. We don't process our learning. We just start over.

In my own busy life, I find myself multi-tasking all day, moving from one thing to another. I don't know if technology has made life easier, but it has certainly made it busier. Ancient monks called the idea of stopping what you are doing, reflecting, and then thinking about the next thing, "statio." This brief interval between things would allow them to focus their energy on the moment. Joan Chittister describes it this way: "Statio is the desire to do consciously what I might otherwise do mechanically." In other words, before I make a phone call, I need to quiet myself and think about the person I am calling, and what I want to say. When a student comes in to talk, I need to stop what I am doing and be in the moment with the student. We need to be aware of and practice "statio." We need to think. So do our students.

Students need to think and talk about what they are learning, throughout the learning process. At the beginning of my class I always tell my students to "focus on English." This means they take a breath, look at their notes, get out materials, and consider what they learned or did yesterday and what we are about to study or do today. Every few minutes in my class, whether we are reading, note-taking, or participating in some activity, I have students stop, talk, connect, and apply. Paraphrasing new information or articulating their own ideas before it all vanishes from their brains locks in the learning.

A benefit of verbal reflection is that by listening to ideas and interpretations and applications of peers, students may understand things better than hearing my version alone. They can make new and more relevant connections, and think in different ways. "By providing students with the opportunity to discuss the topic with each other every ten to fifteen minutes, the students who understand both adult speak and student speak have the opportunity to translate for the students who only speak student." (Cain and Laird, 2011) This "talk to your neighbor" activity is a great way to cause learning, complete understanding, and foster retention. It demands recall, connection, and application. I can assess if students have processed correctly. And they can make their own relevance.

Some teachers have students write in journals in their classrooms at the beginning of class as a bell ringer activity. I suggest using the journal as a reflection notebook at the end of class instead. Allow students time to reflect on the lesson. Provide sentence stems to get them started. These are the daily lesson reflection sentence stems on the wall in my room. Students are encouraged to use them initially, but after a few weeks, during reflection time, they just start writing.

> "Today the lesson was…
> I still have questions about…
> I would like to talk more or know more about…
> The most interesting or significant fact today was…
> An interesting connection to my own life is…
> What I will remember from today's lesson is…
> Summarize today's reading or activity:
> One concept or skill we practiced that I will use regularly is…
> If I only remember one thing today it will be…"

Students are encouraged to use more than one stem if time allows. The purpose of the reflection is two-fold: First, it allows students time to process, synthesize, and apply learning. "Thus, instead of the teacher spending precious time trying to emphasize the relevance of the content to the students (which, in many cases, actually seems to decrease relevance for the student), the teacher simply provides students with the opportunity to create their own relevance." (Cain and Laird, 2011). Students consider not only what they learned, but why it is important and what they will do with it.

Second, this type of reflection, oral or written, provides feedback for the teacher. In addition to the every few minute stop and share reflections in my classroom, or the occasional daily reflections on learning, I also ask students to reflect at the end of a week, unit, grading period, semester or year. What I learn from students then informs my instruction; it tells me how I am doing. Did the learning goals I hoped to achieve happen? What could I omit and for what should I allocate more time? Do units fail or succeed because of content, instruction, or something else? Are students bored, or engaged? Student reflection is helpful for both the student and the teacher.

I shared in an earlier chapter some of my students' reflections on our Shakespeare study. Here are a few more, with my own thought responses in parentheses.

"Memorizing the lines of Shakespeare was fun and I became more familiar with what he has done while I was searching for something I wanted to recite. The audio tapes are cool and I am very glad we are getting to hear the play read as it should be read instead of trying to stumble through reading it aloud as a class." (I wondered if students enjoyed following the audio and discussing the language and events periodically versus reading the play aloud.)

"When an average American like myself starts reading Shakespeare, it's about like reading a bunch of jumbled up words randomly put together. It makes no sense. Then when I sit down and read one line at a time, I realize every line is beautiful. The way he wrote was amazing. He could write about a trash can and the reader would think it was extraordinary." (No way will I use a translated or abridged version.)

"The audio tapes make reading *Macbeth* a thousand times better. I don't stumble over trying to sound out each word, it goes by faster, and it's less confusing with all the different voices. I like all the background information we were given about Shakespeare because it really helps me get a sense of who he was and the time of his writing. It helps me to understand why he wrote certain plays and it also shows how much of an impact he had on everything after." (I was actually thinking of omitting most of the background information in an effort to focus more on skills, so this gave me pause. Perhaps the background serves to create relevance and interest for some students.)

Student reflections can be informative—and rewarding. This one, from a shy student who really had to work to succeed, made me smile: "This year in English 4 has been a pretty good year in the sense that I have learned a lot about myself and how you can make a class fun or boring. I don't think I can forget the time I read the funny play that satirized meeting new people. That play helped me develop into a person who can speak in front of a crowd. Also I grew in writing analysis essays. After reading *Death of a Salesman,* writing the analysis took me a long time, and it was the most nervous I had been about turning in a paper. When I got it back and there was an A at the top I felt proud of myself in knowing I can write a good paper with a little bit of work."

And this: "I will remember the drama section the most. I feel as if the definition of catharsis will never leave my head and I am glad, for it makes me feel smart. I will also remember the cards because the cards are the devil. I feel as if every time I don't know an answer the card with my name on it comes out of the deck. But it's okay because now I am a stronger and more confident person in answering questions out loud."

(Note: The cards to which she refers are the deck of playing cards I keep with each student's name on a card. After we "talk to a neighbor" about something, I randomly pull a card and ask that student to share. Sometimes I'll ask for his or her own thoughts, which are more richly developed after conversing with neighbors; and sometimes, I'll ask a student to share the opinion of someone at the table, which requires that students actively listen and interact with each other. I use the cards to group students, to select "volunteers," and to answer questions; but I try not to put students on the spot without time to prepare before speaking aloud.)

Students learn to connect and apply through reflection. In Samuel Scudder's 1974 classic essay, "Take This Fish and Look at It," he says: "'Facts are stupid things until brought into connection with some general law.'" Consider the story about hunters trapping monkeys by putting barrels that were full of bananas, and had small circular holes cut in the sides, out in the forest. The monkeys would run up to the barrels, stick their arms in the holes, grab a banana, and then could not get their arms out with the bananas in their grasp. Yet they would not let go of the fruit, even when to hold on was dangerous. This is just an interesting story. Except, upon reflection, I thought that English teachers (myself included) are somewhat like this: We don't want to let go of the way we have always done things, the favorite literature or units we teach, even when our standards, technology, students' lives and careers are vastly different than they were twenty years ago. It was only upon reflection that I was able to connect the story, make it a learning moment, and take a hard look at my own curriculum and practices. It became a defining moment in my career, a story I start many presentations with, and something I will never forget.

I want this type of meaning to come from my lessons, for my students. "You can teach what you have always taught.

You can teach it almost the same way you have always taught it. Just add [reflection, and] frequent, small-group, purposeful talk. More of your students will learn more of what you want them to know." (Cain and Laird, 2011). This is what I have found to be true.

Finally, here are some of my student reflections after writing a story or narrative; then reading a story by Hemingway, studying his style, and rewriting their narratives in his style; then reading a story by Faulkner, discussing his style, and rewriting their narratives in Faulkner's style. I introduced this assignment in my first book (*Two Roads Diverged and I Took Both*) as a way to make reading about the writing, and to teach students to analyze and imitate writer style in an effort to inform and enhance their own writing. I love these reflections. Here is where learning happens—when they *realize* what has happened!

"When we first read the short story by Hemingway and there was talk that we were going to have to rewrite our short story like he would, I had a little freak out. I kept thinking, *there is no way I can write like someone else, I can barely write like myself.*"

"Dialogue can be your story; it shows who your characters are or are trying to be without directly telling the reader, which is an exciting way to tell a story. It gives the story more alluring factors, and the readers are always trying to figure who each character is and how they can relate to them. It was a fun assignment that taught me a lot."

"I guess this test of my abilities ended up teaching me that there is always more than one side to a story, in literature as well as in life. There are always different ways to look at something."

"Faulkner's words are very precise and wisely chosen. They seem as if a wise man would say those words, instead of a simple man, like Hemingway's writing. I used a thesaurus to rewrite my Faulkner story."

"When mocking Faulkner, I had to make my brain hurt by trying to use big words and by writing a story in the shape of a block."

"Hemingway's style consists of lots of dialogue which I feel made my story better because the conversations the characters were having internally worked really well externally, too. In my story I feel like every aspect of Hemingway's style complimented my own. The events leading up without the extreme detail you would see from Faulkner made my story more of a surprise. This opens up new opportunities I never have seen before."

"As a seventeen year old when I say 'lots of people' I mean 'lots of people' every time. When I was writing Faulkner's paper I had to use different words for the same meaning, such as 'mob,' 'town,' 'crowd.' All of these could have just been 'lots of people' but Faulkner wouldn't write that way. So I was forced to think and not repeat it over and over again."

If you have ever felt like you are teaching so hard, and so passionately, and no one ever gets it, and then someone really does—a student writes something beautiful, or thanks you for suggesting a book, or falls in love with poetry—you will understand why this next reflection literally brought tears to my eyes, because of the way she wrote it, and because she really got it.

"Hemingway's style is a straight line, a journalist's mark aimed at telling the truth in all its forms. Faulkner leaves an artist's blot on literature, leaving no space for interpretation with deliberate, long, winding sentences. Hemingway's flat dialogue and serious content create undertones of hopelessness that force the reader to unwillingly confront the despairs of life. He quite literally 'speaks' his characters onto the page, using dialogue exclusively for character development, and imagery to convey tone. His words are factual, simple conversations where the speaker is not even always known; the conversational attitude of his writing makes it easy to read, so the reader floats along captured in the story, yet we come upon the ending and realize we have learned of the tragedies of life. It is not until we reflect upon Hemingway's writing that we realize every conversation, every detail, every brief sentence, and long-winded description, have led us to the truth of the story and that of a scarred humanity."

She continues: "Faulkner will lead us, like a tour guide, describing every painful detail, missing no single event, and at the end we have no choice but to know the entire story. Hemingway will run us like a marathon straight through the heart of the story, and we come upon the finish line breathless but understanding. This assignment gave me a purpose: to put every word on trial for its life, to decide whether they live or die for the sake of a story. Imitating Faulkner was not so much of a stretch; I already knew that it was upon detail and imagery that I built my own writing. Writing like Hemingway was a bigger challenge; to leave details out, hurt my heart. I was confronted with the greatest obstacle: what if the reader comes to a different conclusion than I intended? How could I, a dedicated writer, leave it up to them to find the truth in my writing? Together these separate challenges created a more distinct voice of my own. I discovered what I appreciated as a reader, and therefore, as a writer." (Fallon Zollars)

Reflection, both the kind that happens periodically during the learning process, in simple critical writing activities to articulate meaning or in pair or group shares with recall and response, and the kind that happens at the end of a lesson, unit, grading period, or course, is an indispensable learning tool and a very productive use of the time it takes. My students' reflections, in addition to allowing them to really process and apply learning, have informed and improved my instruction more than any teacher training or journal article ever could. I keep a space in my lesson plans to write a quick "note to self" after each class to remind me how it went, for planning purposes. These reflections have made me more aware of everything that happens around me.

And sometimes, they are just funny, such as the one I wrote after a class period recently, during which I completely lost control of my 12th grade boys (in a humorous, not harmful, way). I emailed this to a couple of colleagues for a good laugh:

Me: Today we are going to talk about the characters in the Prologue to *The Canterbury Tales*. Remember yesterday we discussed the background? Get out your notes and books.

A random student: Can we write a screen play where you kill us one by one and no one knows who is doing it?

Another random student: Did you tell us to bring our books? I'm pretty sure I don't know where mine is.

Another random student: Can I go to my locker?

Me: Let's talk about the first character, the knight.

A student: I don't have my notes.

A student: Was he a midget?

Me: What?

A student: Can I borrow a pen? This is only, like, the seventh or eighth time I've asked.

A student: You know, a dwarf.

A student:	I actually don't think you gave me a book. Or someone, like, stole it.
A student:	I prefer short person.
Yet another student:	You know you can rent a midget?
Me:	What are you talking about?
Student:	Yeah, and it's not that expensive to rent one, either.
Me:	Why are we talking about this? Can we get back to *The Canterbury Tales*, please?
Student:	What page are we on?
Student:	Don't ask me. I don't have a book.
Student:	I saw on Facebook that a lot of exes are coming to the basketball tournament.
Student:	I can't wait for the basketball tournament.
Me:	The knight didn't have satire on him, but the squire did. Let's read and see what Chaucer says about the squire.
Student:	Are you coming to the basketball tournament?
Student:	I saw, like, four midgets at HEB the other day. I'm not lying.
Student:	Define midget. Like, do you have to be a certain height to qualify?
Student:	What if there was a basketball game with just midgets?
Me:	(muttering to no one in particular): What is happening?

Student: It says here that the nun is not 'undergrown.'
                     What does that even mean?

Student: If I had a book, I would tell you.

Student: That she's not a midget!

Student (glaring at me): Josh is absent. I think our screen
                     play has already started. Where's Josh???

Student: Hey—Is the monk banging the nun?

I could not make this stuff up.

Notes and Reflection

CHAPTER EIGHT: CONCLUSION

MILES TO GO

The woods are lovely, dark, and deep.

But I have promises to keep,

And miles to go before I sleep,

And miles to go before I sleep.

—Robert Frost, "Stopping
by Woods on a Snowy Evening"

CONCLUSION

MILES TO GO

Recently a young administrator, who had not previously taught English, suggested that I might consider scanning the contents of my file folders in all my file cabinets onto a computer and saving them in something called "the cloud." Bless her heart. She might as well have asked me to throw out all my clothes.

You can imagine the look of incredulity on my face. She is not the first, however, to suggest such a thing. A previous administrator glanced pointedly over at my file cabinets and gave me a flash drive. Now, I ask you, what are the odds that I will lose that flash drive? And what are the odds I will lose the four one-hundred pound file cabinets that sit unobtrusively in the corner in my room? Those file cabinets represent nearly thirty years of work! I *need* my files, because you see, I never know when I might have to teach something again. I never know when a young teacher might want to borrow my notes, lessons, and assignments. I am proud of all the research and lesson planning I did, preparing all my own lessons "from scratch," long before there were programs or services that did this for teachers. I learned so much accumulating those files. So "the cloud" is just not going to happen.

This does bring to light a valid point, however. I, and many experienced teachers, are at an awkward age. If we were younger, we would be digital natives like our students, eager to adapt to the rapid and constant changes in technology in education. We would share the enthusiasm of our young leaders and colleagues when they show us this or that wonderful new gadget or app for grades, lesson plans, required forms, or instruction. We would not grow angry that they assume prior knowledge we do not have and use vocabulary we do not know. If we were younger, we would not spend hours after hours staring through tears at a computer or device that won't work. Finally, we would understand the language of our students when they try to tell us what is wrong with our computer, other than, inevitably, it is "too old to run that program." (Sometimes I just want to say, "So am I, darlin', so am I.")

If we were older, we might say to heck with all this and retire, rather than putting forth the time and effort to learn all the new stuff. And that would be a shame, because while we are not digital natives, we are education natives. There are things we have learned about kids, instruction, leadership, and life that no app can replace. Indeed, I wonder how much time and money has been spent over the years to improve schools and education, when someone probably could have just asked an experienced teacher. We still strive to be the best we can be, and we want to provide the most relevant, engaging and useful instruction for our students—and that means, we will never, ever be able to stop learning.

When I present trainings or give talks for teachers, the greatest fear they express to me is that they will be replaced, that they are not relevant in today's world. I disagree. The processes and products may look different as our students read and write using the technology available today. At some point, a typewriter looked different from a pencil, too. But the cognitive skills of reading and writing must still be taught. The exposure to and ability to understand text is the most incredible gift, regardless of where or how that text is presented. We get to give our students the best things to read that we know, and guide them through to understanding. We get to unlock their ability to organize and articulate complex thought, and express it effectively and correctly. Indeed, to write is to have a voice in this world and believe that it matters. We can still do this for our students. We will always be needed. We will always be relevant.

I have learned that when fear, or uncertainty, or change knocks on the door, I have to get faith to answer it. I have learned that it is only through stretching that I grow, and only through trying several things that I find the ones worth keeping. I have learned to never shut the door on something just because it's new or out of my comfort zone, but not to let everything that knocks, take up residence. I have learned that the skills I teach my students will impact their lives far more than the content I use to teach them, and that teaching writing and reading are active, intense, engaging processes. I should be, and am, tired at the end of an instructional day. But it's a "good tired." I know that passion is contagious; that grace saves more minds than justice; that feedback causes learning; and that reflection solidifies that learning and leads to application, which can change lives. I know that teachers can, and do, change lives.

Yes, teaching English is hard work, but such a blessing. Author Anne Lamott says the two best prayers she knows are "Help me, help me, help me," and "Thank you, thank you, thank you." And one of these, I think, is every teacher's prayer on any given day. It is cliché I know, but I find the more I know about teaching, the more I realize I don't know, and the more I *want* to know; and that passion, above all else, has made me a better teacher. I said I wish I had had this book when I began, but then, the magic carpet ride would have been different. The bumps and dives are part of it, after all. I have taught for twenty-seven years. I have a lot of files. I won some awards. I have miles to go.

Notes and Reflection

AFTERWORD

FROM MELANIE MAYER CONSULTING

"My candle burns at both ends. It will not last the night. But ah, my foes, and oh, my friends—it gives a lovely light."

—Edna St. Vincent Millay

FROM MELANIE MAYER CONSULTING
(FACEBOOK POSTS)

August 17, 2012

"I have spread my dreams under your feet;
Tread softly because you tread on my dreams." —William
Butler Yeats

As we head back to school I am reminded of what a blessing it is to be an English teacher. Though certainly grading
essays is time-consuming, these words are gifts our students

give to us. Our gift to them is our response. We exchange gifts in the ELA classroom all day long. This is our special blessing. Our students come to us in all grade levels with their dreams spread out before them. Good luck this year. Expect much, tread softly, be blessed.

August 23, 2012

On Monday our speaker John Perricone talked about the Chinese idea of "Sho Shin"—which means "fresh mind." His point was to cherish your beginner's mind, cherish the way you were when you first began. Remember how you felt when you first became a parent, or a Christian. Revisit that. Start each day with fresh eyes. I love that idea as it applies to teaching. See students as if we are beginning teachers, with that enthusiasm, that idealism. Learn new things. See each class, even the last of the day, with your first mind, fresh mind. This is going to be a great year!

August 31, 2012

Back to school! I am teaching four classes at the high school, two at Del Mar College in the evenings, and am traveling to present several teacher trainings in the coming months. I also have a couple articles set for publication, and on weekends, am loading the boat with fish and working hard (well, not really) to get my golf handicap down. My well-meaning friends comment that I am trying to do too much, always on the go—"burning the candle at both ends." I am reminded of the poem by Edna St. Vincent Millay: "My candle burns at both ends. It will not last the night. But ah, my foes, and oh, my friends—it gives a lovely light." Light 'em up, colleagues!

September 29, 2012

One of the skills that I love teaching my students is to think about the writer when they read, and think about the reader when they write. Students who have grown up in the "No Child Left Behind" era must be taught that reading is not just about locating information. It is how a writer moves, carries, and manipulates us. When it works, we must examine rhetorical choices to determine why. Likewise, students must be taught that their writing it not just about/ for them; on the contrary, they must be ever-conscious of their readers as they make choices as writers. As English teachers, we know (and now, EOC demands) that we must get in the kitchen and examine how writers "make it."

October 12, 2012

Mihaly Csikszentmihalyi, a Hungarian emigrant and psychologist, professor, and writer, is most noted for his work on a condition called "flow": "the mental state of operation in which a person performing an activity is fully immersed in a feeling of energized focus, full involvement, and enjoyment." I am picturing my classroom in just that state! How exciting would that be! He says "Enjoyment appears at the boundary between boredom and anxiety, when the challenges are just balanced with the person's capacity to act." Interestingly, the best definition of rigorous instruction I have come across says almost the same thing: challenges should be just beyond the periphery of the student's present knowledge and ability. Things can't be too easy or they are bored; they can't be unreachable or they give up. The right amount of rigor in the classroom makes learning enjoyable, and creates "flow." Woo-hoo!

October 24, 2012

A man driving his car on a very tall bridge noticed another man standing out on the very top, about to jump, which would result in his certain death. The Good Samaritan quickly pulled over, and rushed out to the would-be jumper, to try and talk him out of jumping. "It can't be that bad," he said. "Tell me about it." For the next three hours, the first guy did exactly that. When he finished, they both jumped. Spread some joy, folks, spread some joy!

October 25, 2012

When we learn something new, if we don't have a reason and opportunity to use it immediately and often, we forget it. This is also true with our students, and was made clear to me recently when our librarian taught them to use Dropbox, Google Docs, and our online data bases. I gave them a follow-up assignment that required them to use the information the next day, knowing if I didn't, some that could benefit from it and love it would never even take time—or have time—to try it. And if they needed it sometime in the future, they would have forgotten the knowledge. This is true with any skill we teach in the classroom: if we really want students to learn it, they have to regularly reflect on and connect their learning, and practice the skill. We can't just store things away and expect to remember it all. We have to use it, or lose it.

Today I asked my students to finish an assignment they started in my class yesterday. Over half of them pulled it up on Google Docs. Hooray for learning!

October 31, 2012

Robert Cormier said, "The beautiful part of writing is that you don't have to get it right the first time, unlike, say, a brain surgeon. You can always do it better, find the exact word, the apt phrase, the leaping simile." I love the grace of an art—and a life—that allows for continuous revision. I should have, I could have, I would have. Erase. Delete. Revise. We're good.

November 11, 2012

I received some startling information from a colleague in Florida last week: NAEP administered the first computer-based writing assessment in 2011 to 25,000 8th and 12th graders. The data about students' use of writing technology was revealing. The test tracked the technology tools the students could have used on the test. Less than 20% of both 8th and 12th graders ever used the Cut, Copy, Paste tools at any time! How did they revise???? Lack of computers is not the problem. 87% had operational computers at home. They spend countless hours online—but these hours are not spent doing formal writing or formatting papers in Word. In other academic classes they use technology—iPads, for example—but not to write formal papers. It is not the same. This is a literacy deficiency! We must recognize our new roles as English teachers in this era. If we are not teaching them some of the simple rules and tools for writing on the computer, they will not learn them, and their progress through high school and into college will be hindered.

November 26, 2012

I absolutely love the NCTE convention. I am so humbled by the intelligence in any given room there. That so many brilliant, kind, compassionate, literate, inspiring people have devoted their lives to teaching validates the profession for me once again. Most teachers just really have a passion not only for their subject, but for people, and education, and philosophy, and learning. I was given more food for thought than I can even digest, including great ideas for my own classroom, and great things to consider about life. After all, as Neil DeGrasse Tyson puts it:

"My view is that if your philosophy is not unsettled daily then you are blind to all the universe has to offer."

November 29, 2012

"The purpose of education has changed from that of producing a literate society to that of producing a learning society." Margaret Ammons, Associate Secretary of ASCD, October 1964 Wow. I thought this was another quote about how today's students need to be taught skills and not content, how to do things, how to adapt, how to learn for themselves and not just regurgitate information—how we need to prepare them better for college, for jobs they will have that aren't even invented yet. Then I saw the date. We must always be a learning society. We have always been. Just sometimes we are learning different things, and at a different pace.

December 5, 2012

I recently read a report that most teachers spend more time preparing for direct teaching, such as lecture, than they do for activities. If there is time left in class, they will do an activity that supports the "learning." However, observations prove that most student engagement and learning actually takes place during the activities, not during direct teach. We should actually spend more time planning and preparing activities for students in which they are engaged in actively learning; then if there is time, we can fill in gaps and support with direct teach/review. This "backwards" model takes time to plan and more time to get used to, but I love the enthusiasm, initiative, and especially the learning, that is taking place in my classroom.

December 6, 2012

Peg Tyre's article, "The Writing Revolution" in The Atlantic (2012) is so good I am posting a link to it. It validates two things I have always believed: 1. We must actively teach all students how to write — not just inspire them and put them in a writing environment, but teach them solid essay structure and the components of language and make them do it until they can. And 2. Writing is the way students demonstrate learning. If they cannot write, they will be wrongly judged, labeled, ignored, and deprived of the keys to everything they want and deserve in this life. This is a fantastic read and worth the time!

December 12, 2012

"It is essential for you—for me—to have something significant yet to do—to have a positive vision of our future—because that is what gives meaning to life."—from Joel Barker's *The Power of Vision*

I think having a vision of the future—believing we have something significant yet to do—is partly what makes good teachers—or leaders in any field—great. And if we think about the power of passion, and vision, and hope in a future in our own lives, we cannot help but realize that we must help our students—all our students—see and believe in a future of significance in their own lives.

December 22, 2012

I asked my students after a recent test to write brief reflections on their learning in English 4 Dual Credit— their first semester of college English. One student commented: "Learning to revise effectively has been the most valuable tool. Revision is not as simple as I originally thought and learning to make a paper better AFTER it is written is a skill I now value greatly." Another said: "I have learned things I will carry with me for the rest of my life. I am working on making my writing more clear and understandable for the reader." Still another wrote: "I have learned you can learn to write by reading what other people have written!" And finally, "More than anything, this class has given me confidence that I can do it." I am so thankful for these Christmas blessings. Merry Christmas to all.

January 7, 2013

"Real teaching is patience and courage and endurance and perception. It drowns the teacher. But then, so does anything done well."—Pam Brown

As I prepare to get back into the grind at work after a holiday break, I find that after all these years what I am most concerned with is how I can do something more this semester to challenge and prepare my students. I am constantly looking for better material, better methods, more patience, more creativity—and sometimes, truly, trying to be a great teacher feels like drowning. How many times we (English teachers) have said, "I am drowning in work!" And it feels like that. But we aren't victims. We are heroes. We drown so they can swim. Flail those arms, kick those legs. Dive on in. Happy 2013.

January 12, 2013

"To live a single day and hear good teaching is better than to live a hundred years without knowing such teaching." Buddha

January 14, 2013

Check out the poem, "Poetry" by Pablo Neruda. So beautiful. Teachers: use it with an excerpt from Malcolm X's autobiography (I like "Literacy Behind Bars") to compare tones, themes, and rhetoric across genres. One speaker is freed by literacy; one by poetry. Poetic Souls: just read it to remember how you, too, were once "summoned, from the branches of night, abruptly from the others, among violent fires…" when "poetry arrived in search of [you]."

January 30, 2013

In John Perricone's Zen and the Art of Public School Teaching, he quotes a colleague who sums up what I believe experience teaches all of us: "The first twenty-five years of my career I taught [English]—the last five years I taught people. What a difference it made in my life and the lives of my students." Standardized testing doesn't change this. If anything, it brings even more to the forefront the need to teach people what they need to know to enrich and empower their own lives. More often than not, this is not content. After all, I don't want to know how the iPad works; I just want to use it!

February 6, 2013

I just read Katherine Boo's *Beyond the Beautiful Forevers*, about life in a Mumbai Undercity, a slum in India next to an airport. I sat stunned after reading this, at the gap between those who have and those who have nothing. It reminds me of the time my student from India went back to visit, and was so moved she determined to make it her life's work to change something there. She described opulence and penury as existing side by side, and could not understand how this was possible.

And yet, doesn't that happen here as well? Truly, there are excerpts from this non-fiction masterpiece worth sharing with our students, from both a human and literary perspective.

February 8, 2013

"I've seen how you can't learn anything when you're trying to look like the smartest person in the room." A student shared that this week as one of his favorite lines from *The Poisonwood Bible*, the beautiful novel by Barbara Kingsolver my dual credit students are reading right now. It's so true: we've all had that athlete that was talented but not "coachable," or the student who was brilliant, but would not grow. This quote reminds me also to be quiet and listen, and learn from those around me, old and young, big and small.

February 13, 2013

"I'll Take the Zero"

I am having lunch with several of my seniors this week, much to their dismay. I am not convinced they did their best work—or, any work—on a recent major essay assignment. Several of them decided they would rather "take the zero." So, we are having lunch together this week, until the assignment is complete.

I told them I can't let them "take a zero." They asked me: "Why do you care? We aren't going to college. This isn't a dual credit class. We don't need to write these essays." But I can't limit them like that, or allow them to limit themselves. They do not know right now what they may be doing in the future. I have to prepare them for all possibilities. It's my job.

And suddenly, it hits me: There are a lot of times I don't want to learn or do something new that is hard. I would rather "take the zero, too!"

But I do it for my students. They are why I can't limit myself, when it would be so much easier to do so. They make me better. And so, why are we having lunch? I am returning the favor.

February 21, 2013

I am not a huge fan of Walt Whitman's poetry. But I am a fan of Pablo Neruda's poetry. And he credits Walt Whitman as his inspiration. Most people on the street could not say who Henry David Thoreau was. But they know who Gandhi was, and Martin Luther King, Jr., and both were inspired by Thoreau. I shared this with my students and it really seemed to make them appreciate the "originals" more. Also, it reinforces that we do not know what our legacy will be. Our biggest influence as teachers may not be immediate or visible to us. But there is a student, who will do great things one day, and touch many, many lives, as many as Pablo or Martin or Mahatma, and he/she may well say, "I had a teacher…"

February 26, 2013

From time to time we need to ask our students: "What can I do to help you be successful in my class?" Give them time to think about this question and require a response.

Recently a student shared with me that as a slow reader, when we read a story or article in class and then talk about it, she is never finished with the reading. It was one of those moments when you slap your head at your own stupidity. She suggested I give her the articles or stories the day before so she can "get a head start." To use my mom's expression: "Shoot a mile!" Why didn't I think of this? From now on, I will give all my students the articles or stories for the next day in advance (or post them), and those that want to "get a head start" can do that.

March 4, 2013

In a great article in Educational Leadership this month, "Students First, Not Stuff," Will Richardson suggests that educators today need to focus more on "developing kids who are 'learners' instead of trying to make sure they're 'learned.'" Kids today do not need a store of information readily available in memory; there is not an information shortage! Instead, they need "the skills and dispositions necessary for them to learn whatever they need to learn whenever they need to learn it." This "disposition" he speaks of is a propensity for lifelong learning—a desire to learn, to adapt, to persevere, to adjust, and to grow for the sake of something important to the individual. Instead of making kids "college ready," we might benefit more from making them "learning ready," prepared for any opportunity. And we ourselves must remain "learning ready" and model this for them.

March 8, 2013

I was asked recently if assessments in Texas have changed the way I teach. The short answer is no. But assessments promote a greater awareness, and awareness has changed the way I teach: I am aware of specific stated standards, and constantly think on the best way to teach them to my students. I am aware that what my students can do is more important than what I know. I am aware of the benefit to me of online and paper journals, articles, books, research, and workshops on leadership, management, pedagogy, and instruction. I am aware of the power of reflection, and of my students' potential, and their overwhelming desire to succeed, however disguised. Assessments, and experience, have made me more aware—and that awareness, over the last few years, has changed the way I teach.

March 19, 2013

My dual credit class sent me to spring break with a gift: They did a beautiful job on an in-class assignment. I had them read "The Public Thinker" by Bob Herbert, a tribute to Arthur Miller, author of *The Crucible* and *Death of a Salesman*. I reminded them how readers approach non-fiction, mentally participating in the discussion set forth in the text, underlining, taking notes, thinking. I had them write a concise summary of the article, and then an academic response/analysis. These are college readiness and life-enhancing skills we have been refining all year. I was so proud of their mental engagement with the text and the depth of their responses. Some students tentatively—or boldly, depending on their level of academic confidence—challenged Herbert's positions, or his rhetorical choices; others enthusiastically applauded them. One student endeared himself to me forever by exclaiming "Alack, this makes me want to cry!" The writer's warning, ironically, is that we must not lose the ability to think—which is in fact the very purpose of this assignment, and, I think, education as a whole.

March 20, 2013

"Do you want to see my tattoo?" My students snicker, for this newly acquired (spring break) and scandalous tattoo on one of my student's rear end is the subject of much discussion. Not unless it's a picture of your college diploma.

March 21, 2013

"Be the people your parents think you are." I scolded—encouraged (?)—my senior class recently. As a teacher, one of the greatest gifts I can give my students is to see them—and treat them—as their very best selves. It is my responsibility—and privilege—to see them as they can become, and to push and prepare them for lives, careers, responsibilities, and blessings they cannot currently imagine having.

March 25, 2013

"For students, critical writing creates meaning, solidifies connections, transforms subconscious ideas into conscious thoughts, and is essential for authentic literacy." (Cain and Laird, The Fundamental Five: The Formula for Quality Instruction, 23) Critical writing demands that students articulate what they think—which means they must first participate in actively thinking about what they know. Purposeful, organized writing is the beginning of academia, and one of the most crucial skills we teach.

April 2, 2013

Teachers hang on to the best student products: the best essay, the best poem. We keep the good stuff to use as mentor texts for our students each coming year: here is how you do it; here is an example of a really good one. Students like seeing previous students' work. It empowers them and inspires them.

It recently occurred to me that a worthy goal as a teacher is to have a new "best ever" every year!

April 8, 2013

Great teaching tip: "By providing students with the opportunity to discuss with each other the topic at hand every ten to fifteen minutes, the students who understand both adult speak and student speak have the opportunity to translate for the students who only speak student." (Cain and Laird, *The Fundamental Five: The Formula for Quality Instruction*, 54) Whether you call it "talk to a neighbor" or "pair share" or something else, the idea is that students must recall and articulate and connect learning. I do this every single day.

Here are concrete examples from last week's classes:

"Talk to your neighbor and identify three adjectives that best describe the protagonist. Two minutes and we'll share whole group."

"Talk to your neighbor: what new information did the video clip provide about the Renaissance?"

"Talk in small groups for a minute: why did Marlow lie to Kurtz's fiancé about his last words?"

"Talk to your neighbor: how did Conrad's use of imagery contribute to the tone and theme of the story?"

I follow up the short talks with whole group discussion, critical writing, or we simply move on. Everyone gets to have a voice—those who were lost in the lesson are found, or redirected, and learning is solidified. "You can teach what you have always taught. You can teach it almost the same way you have always taught it. Just add frequent, small-group, purposeful talk. More of your students will learn more of what you want them to know." (Cain and Laird, *The Fundamental Five*, 68)

April 9, 2013

Why Jane Austen will always be relevant:

"Have you seen any pleasant men? Have you had any flirting?"—Lydia, in *Pride and Prejudice*

"The more I know of the world, the more I am convinced that I shall never see a man whom I can really love. I require so much!"—Marianne, in *Sense and Sensibility*

April 10, 2013

Why Jane Austen will always be relevant, Part 2:

"Poverty is a great evil, but to a woman of education and feeling it ought not, it cannot be the greatest. I would rather be a teacher at a school (and I can think of nothing worse) than marry a man I did not like."—Emma in *The Watsons*

April 11, 2013

Two book recommendations, because even teachers have to make time to read something just for ourselves: Read *The Elegance of the Hedgehog,* by Muriel Barbery. This is the kind of book you have to reach up and get, that you are smarter for reading—not just in the head but in the heart. Read *The Fifteen Invaluable Laws of Growth*, by John C.

Maxwell. Unfulfilled potential is like dying with the music still inside you. This, and other ideas, and tons of quotable quotes are set forth in this book for those of us committed to continual personal growth.

April 15, 2013

"I have one life and one chance to make it count for something...My faith demands that I do whatever I can, wherever I am, whenever I can, for as long as I can with whatever I have to try to make a difference." —Jimmy Carter

May 1, 2013

Teachers are asked to "differentiate" in the classroom: to teach all students at their own levels, according to their own learning styles, pace, needs, and personalities. The idea is to challenge all students, with different levels of materials and tasks.

This is not hard, if you have the right mindset. Differentiation is life. This is what great coaches (and great leaders in any field) do. They treat all players differently, teaching them to reach beyond their ability level and improve, motivating some through glaring, others through praise, still others through a sharp word. (Here my ex-athletes who read this are saying, "And others, through running." LOL)

Great teaching is like great coaching. We have a game plan; we will "win" some lessons or class days, and we lose some.

But what really matters are the players. We differentiate to engage stars, motivate slackers, improve weaknesses, maximize strengths, celebrate growth, and give each "player" things that will last after the letter jackets wear out.

May 10, 2013

Yesterday in class when I asked my seniors to get out their notebooks and review their reflections from the previous day, one student asked if he could go get his "note page" from his locker. Apparently, a "note page" is what substitutes for a notebook when one is completely unorganized and just writes the notes for each day on borrowed bits and pieces of paper, and then crams them into a book, bag, pocket, or locker.

So today, when I asked students to turn in their homework, the same student said his homework seemed not to be in his portfolio, and could he please go to his locker and search for it. "Portfolio?" I asked. He held up a fifteen cent folder with pockets, which held in it, one note page.

Another student said, "I can't find my homework, either. For some reason, it's not in my bag." I glanced over to see him searching through a torn and worn-looking plastic HEB grocery bag, which held pencils, candy, a book (not English), random handouts from various classes, a phone, and several "note pages," but no homework.

I sometimes don't know whether to laugh or cry.

Help me, help me, help me.

June 16, 2013

A headline in the paper today rubbed me wrong: "Lacking Lesson Plans, Students Suffer." In this article, school administrators bemoan the sudden removal of C-Scope lessons. How about this: "Lacking trust and respect, teacher morale suffers."

I have written my own lessons my entire career. Years of college preparation, hundreds of hours of staff development trainings, mentor teachers, knowing the TEKS for my assignment backwards and forwards, continuing to stay abreast and informed of all available resources and research in English Education, and staying in touch with my students, is more than enough empowerment to write engaging, rigorous lessons. In fact, I believe I am a much better teacher because of the time I have spent designing my own lessons to best meet the needs of all my students, each year.

I know there are those, including many of my own respected colleagues, who have used C-Scope lessons with success. That is probably because research shows the single most important thing affecting student achievement is the teacher—not a program, curriculum, budget, or trend.

It's not the end of the world not to have C-Scope lessons. But not to have good teachers—now that might be the end of the world.

June 16, 2013

Some of you have asked me to share my reading list, or at least, the books I read that I would recommend. I wonder: How do I know a book is good? Sometimes it's that I can't put it down. But sometimes, it's that I have to put it down and think.

The Light Between Oceans, by M. L. Stedman, and *The Atonement Child,* by Francine Rivers (who also wrote the most beautiful book, *Redeeming Love*), were good. I know this, because I could feel the pain of the characters in my gut. I literally hurt for these people I didn't know, wept for them, and dreamed about them. And I contemplated what I would do if faced with the issues the books presented.

I realize—this is good writing. And the next logical leap for an English teacher—and her students—is to consider *why.* How did these writers evoke such responses in me? This is what I want to teach my students.

June 27, 2013

This summer, sharpen the saw:

Two guys were cutting down trees. They worked for hours doing this. One said he was going to take a break and sharpen his saw. The other continued to work right through lunch. The first man returned with a sharper saw and cut down twice as many trees.

This summer—sharpen your saw. Take a vacation to get rejuvenated; read inspiring or practical articles about education, teaching, or your field; search the web for another way to do something; or just pick up a great book and remember why you love to read. Go to a conference; talk to the best teacher you know; rewrite your old course outlines or lessons. Find a way to work smarter, more efficiently, more passionately.

I pretend every school year is New Year's Eve, a time to make resolutions and begin again with a new heart and an eager, open mind. From time to time we all just need to sharpen the saw.

July 3, 2013

I have been trying for two years to have time, even one full, quiet day, to work on my next book. I have been so busy teaching, traveling and presenting trainings, that when I do have a day off, I just want to fish or golf—not sit at a desk.

I was rather in despair of not having had time to write this summer, when suddenly I read a quote by Henry David Thoreau: "How vain it is to sit down to write when you have not stood up to live."

July 9, 2013

"The essential element in personal magnetism is a consuming sincerity—an overwhelming faith in the importance of the work one has to do." from Beau Barton, *The Man Nobody Knows*

How blessed I am to have this work that matters, these hobbies, this life. The book will come when it does—or it won't. But I am reluctant to set aside the living for it.

July 19, 2013

So you don't like everything about your job?? There's a support group for that! It's called "everybody." They meet at the bar. Ha ha ha.

But seriously, I think of this as the "Rule of 10 and 2." We all can probably list ten things we like, or are grateful for, about our jobs. But the two things we don't like, tend to be the things we talk about, or focus our minds on. And it's human nature to magnify what we focus on. Problems get bigger and bigger the more we talk about them. What if we magnify the 10 and not the 2?

For example, one thing I love about my job is that I get to wear flip flops. (Settle down; they are "dress" flip flops!) So when the paperwork or pressure gets to be too much, I can just say to myself, "But at least I get to wear flip flops."

There is a choice for every conversation: "I have to be here at 7:30? That's too early! I can't get up that early. I will be grumpy! No one should have to go to work at that time. Can you all believe we have to do this?"

Or, "Well, at least we get to wear flip flops."

July 21, 2013

Get rid of the "buts." We kill our joy with the "buts." For example:

"I am grateful for my job, but…"

"I like so and so, but…."

"These students are pretty smart, but…"

Remember the Bible story of the spies who went to scout out the Promised Land? Ten of them reported: "The fruit is amazing, BUT the giants are scary." "The land is beautiful, BUT there are too many giants." "The promise is magnificent, BUT the problems are too big." Two of them (Caleb and Joshua, if you are looking for inspiring names to give your children) said, "The land is amazing. The fruit is unbelievable. It's worth it."

Make a conscious effort to leave the "buts" out of thoughts and conversation. And if one sneaks in, repeat the statement aloud and leave it out, and note the difference in how you feel and how others react. No "buts" allowed!!

July 28, 2013

My last post was "Get rid of the 'buts'."

I am thinking that is also a good rule for our students:

"I would have studied, but…"

"I did my homework, but…"

"I would have been here, but…"

"I read it, but…"

I think I'll make a poster for my wall that reminds my students and me that what any of us would have done or thought or said is trumped by the evidence. So, "No buts allowed."

And—it could be a good lesson on puns, as well!

August 4, 2013

Those of us who have been in education for any length of time have to smile at the "ever-shifting certainty" we have weathered: open classrooms; inclusion; ability grouping; cooperative learning; process writing; college readiness; No Child Left Behind; vocational training; co-teaching; professional learning communities (PLC); balanced literacy; and flipped classrooms; just to name a few.

And yet, research shows the single most important factor affecting student learning, more than budgets, materials, initiatives, or "programs," is the teacher. Perhaps that is because we are somehow able to stay grounded in knowing what best practices are for our classroom and our students, and we will always do our best, sometimes aided by the trends that come and go, and sometimes in spite of them.

Now is a good time to reflect on what you believe and know to be true about your philosophy of teaching, and what constitutes best practices for the students in your classroom. At the end of the day, great teachers cause learning and growth in young people, and that weighty responsibility is noble, and exciting. I, for one, am ready to rock it out!

August 5, 2013

One of the motivational presentations I offer is called "The Top Ten Signs You Might Be a Great Teacher." I thought it would be fun to post these as we get ready to head back into the classroom. (Of course, without the stand-up routine they won't be near as entertaining.)

Number Ten: You might be a great teacher if you organize and plan instruction. In a great teacher's classroom, nothing happens randomly. Even chaos is planned. Because teaching is not about hope; it's about intentional instruction. Anticipate mistakes your students will make and plan what to do about them. Plan what you will do for the students who don't get it the first time, and for those who had it before you said a word. Even if you are not inclined to organize and plan much outside of school, great teachers know this kind of proactive organization in the classroom breeds clarity, power, and efficiency.

August 7, 2013

Number Nine, Part 1: You might be a great teacher if you have a "yes" face. There is a story about Thomas Jefferson and an army of men standing on the edge of the raging Potomac, preparing to go across. An old hobo lying on the banks of the river got up and walked up to Jefferson and asked him to carry him across. One of the army generals said to the hobo: "Good grief, man, there are hundreds of us here. Why in the world did you choose the president to ask to carry you across??" The hobo said, "Because he was the only one with a 'yes' face."

I can immediately think of certain co-workers of mine who have a "Yes" face. They are approachable and accessible. Adults and students alike are not afraid to ask them for advice, or help, or grace. They make every person feel like there is nothing they would rather do than be in that moment, with that person.Unfortunately, all too often my own face is busy, distracted, or intense. I am going to work on this. Having a "yes" face is really just part of the bigger picture: Great teachers value relationships.

Do you have a "yes" face?

August 9, 2013

Number Nine, Part 2: Great teachers value relationships.

You might be a great teacher if you recognize the value of relationships: with students, with students' parents, and with colleagues. Sometimes grace inspires students more than justice. Sometimes a positive phone call is the greatest gift we can give their parents. Let's make a point to share with parents some of the many things our students do right, whether it's being kind, or going the extra mile on an assignment. Establish rapport early; if you have to make a different kind of phone call later in the year, it will be much better received. Build relationships with colleagues through demonstrating mutual respect, a shared vision, and consistent adherence to school policies.

And remember that a "yes" face is one way to show you value relationships!

August 11, 2013

Number Eight: Great teachers sit with their students in assemblies. WHAT??

When I heard a speaker say this at a conference, I was appalled. I would much rather stand in the back (we do tend to congregate—be honest) and complain about how the students act during an assembly, than SIT WITH THEM. "Just look at these kids. Nobody makes them behave. They are texting. They aren't paying attention." And so on. But great teachers are solutionaries. They won't offer up a problem without also offering up -or implementing- a solution. Not only can we pick out students we know are likely to be distracted, and thus, be a distraction, and sit with them, we can make them feel like we sit there not to discipline, but because we enjoy them. Doing this one little thing makes so many things better, for so many people. What a concept.

August 13, 2013

Number Seven: Great teachers view discipline differently.

1. We need to establish expectations and principles, not rules. Outlining consequences just outlines OPTIONS for some students.
2. Great teachers want prevention, not revenge. We must view discipline as a way to CHANGE behavior, not make students mad!
3. Great teachers don't yell, argue, or use sarcasm. You can't make people angry and sell them something at the same time. I know many teachers think sarcasm is funny. But I always worry that it isn't funny to students who don't understand it, or are sensitive. And it undermines an atmosphere of mutual respect; students who use sarcasm would, after all, be thought of as disrespectful.

Discipline can be a proactive way of life more than a reaction to something bad!

August 17, 2013

Number SIX: Great Teachers Emphasize Skills Over Content

We English teachers are a smart group. We know a lot of stuff. We have read a lot of books. We have FILES. So the idea that what my students learn and can do matters more than what I know is rather disconcerting. It means the actual skills we teach our students are more important than the content we use to get there. I find myself now putting everything I plan and teach through a mental test: How does this benefit, enrich, or empower my students for their purposes? What skills are strengthened by this lesson? Like a coach, I want to constantly see measurable improvement in my students' reading and writing skills, and so I will try to plan accordingly.

Because great teachers know (sigh): it's not about me.

August 21, 2013

Number Five: Great Teachers Accept Responsibility

Although it is easy sometimes to blame other things—the parents rap music adhd drugs class size budget poor administration lack of materials don't get paid enough no discipline in the office cscope athletics bad batch this year worst group I ever had come through — great teachers focus on what they CAN do instead.

Statements like "this is the worst group we've ever had" let teachers off the hook: if students perform poorly, well, I told you so. If they do well in spite of their label, well, I'm a genius. Imagine if you took a car to the shop and the service manager said, "Well, I'll take it and charge you, but I doubt there's anything I can do. 2012 was just a real bad year for cars. Worst group I've seen in years. And we've had these budget cuts. How could you bring it to me in this condition?" When things don't go so well in their classroom or their students aren't successful, great teachers don't cast blame. They just quietly try something else.

August 23, 2013

"Today, kids, we will learn the silent "e" sound. Anna, put down that novel and pay attention!"

Number Four: Great Teachers challenge their students! Learning is like weight lifting: you have to lift enough weight to gain strength. The weights can't be too heavy, but they must be heavy enough that you have to struggle a little to finish, or you won't build muscle. This is the zone, where learning takes place—when the work is not so hard our students can't do it, but hard enough that it requires effort! It is hard to find that place for every student, true; but then, no one ever said great teaching was easy!

August 25, 2013

Number Three: Great Teachers understand the value of reflection.

Experience is not the best teacher; evaluated experience is. Great teachers constantly examine why things went the way they did in each class. Leave room on your lesson plans to make quick notes at the end of a class or a day, of things that were hugely successful, things that fell flat, humorous or poignant moments, and new ideas. We have to reflect on and question everything: planning, instruction, practice, assessment.

Likewise, reflection is a great learning tool for our students as well. It is when we allow them time to process, recall, and think about their learning that they are able to connect it and apply it for their own purposes. There are many ways this can look in your classroom: Think, Pair, Share, "Talk to a Neighbor," end of class reflection journals, or reflections on assessments. I have reflection questions posted on the wall: What was the most significant thing I learned today? How will today's lesson apply to my life? What do I still have questions about? What will I remember, and use again?

Use student reflections—and your own—to inform instruction.

August 27, 2013

Number Two: Great Teachers are passionate!

Passionate teachers are like thermostats, not thermometers: they don't just record the temperature in a room; they change the temperature in a room. Passion is contagious.

The teachers and colleagues I have respected most over the years—and have seen students respect most—are those that are passionate about what they do. Whether it's a coach, band director, math teacher, or something else, the number one thing that seems to make teachers successful in their programs is their passion. I have seen One Act Play coaches who could inspire students to give up spring break to practice every day. I have seen math teachers who could inspire students to give up Saturdays to attend academic competitions. The best of these are not even just passionate about their own field, but are passionate about education and learning in general. If you are at a place where you have lost your passion for teaching—or for whatever it is you do in life—you can get it back. I will tell you how—Friday. It's the number one Sign You Might be a Great Teacher… Stay Tuned!

August 30, 2013

NUMBER ONE SIGN YOU MIGHT BE A GREAT TEACHER: Great Teachers Never Stop Learning!

We can learn from journals, workshops and conferences, observing and talking to colleagues, trial and effort, and reflection. Lifelong learning is a decision; it's a state of mind which includes openness to new ideas and a realization that the way I do something may not be the only or best way. We must not let success be a reason to discontinue growth. It may not be broke, but how long will it serve as the world changes? And how can we make it better? I love to learn new ideas for my own classroom. I have already tried something this week I just learned this summer, from another teacher at a school where I was presenting. Just as we challenge our students, we must challenge ourselves to stay fresh and passionate, and the best way to do that is to keep learning and growing.

September 25, 2013

What I learned by paying attention to my students:

I was helping a struggling, resistant student with a difficult online English class. I kept insisting he "slow down," because he would advance the slide and immediately select and hit "submit" while I was still reading the directions! Finally, exasperated, he told me that because he plays video games all the time, he has learned to "read" the whole screen at once. He's right. When I was in about 4th grade, I was taught to speed read with a big screen and a projector. The teacher flashed text on the screen for seconds, and I would have to tell her what it said. We started with sentences, then short paragraphs, and eventually I was reading whole pages in seconds.

I am happy to know there is one good thing that can come from these video games. However, upon closer examination, I saw this student was scanning the examples and picking the answer that looked like them; there was no real retention of the content or skill. He was playing a video game: go fast and try not to get blown up (wrong answer). If you do, just start over. So this online speed reading thing, though amazing, is not perfect. I also realized: today's students are really smart, regardless of their "labels." They are just smart in a different way than we were smart.

October 7, 2013

In an article in The Wall Street Journal, "Why Tough Teachers Get Good Results," JoAnne Lipman reported new research that supports the following: Strict discipline and explicit instruction get better results than cooperative learning and begging. The old fashioned drill and skill (think spelling words and multiplication tables) works. Immersion into a discipline leads to creativity in that discipline—not the other way around. Grit trumps talent—so we should value and praise work ethic over ability. Finally, failure and stress are good for kids.

November 8, 2013

Teachers are Coaches!

This year the last student who calls me "Coach Mayer" will graduate. True, I have not coached the Lady Marlins since I moved from the basketball court to the English classroom ten years ago. But during the fourteen years I did coach at Port A, I coached his sisters; thus, he has always known me as "Coach." I am going to miss that.

The word "coach" derives from horse-drawn coaches, developed in the town of Kocs during the fifteenth century to transport royalty. Kevin Hall writes in Aspire: "A coach remains something, or someone, who carries a valued person from where they are to where they want to be." I would add this: whether they know they want to be there or not. I believe great teachers are coaches. We have to be meticulous planners, perceptive differentiators, and great motivators. We teach fundamentals and strategies for success in our subject areas, and also for life. As an English teacher, the only thing I can't do that a coach does is make students run laps.

Although now that I think about it…

November 13, 2013

Today as I was grading papers (imagine) I was once again moved by the quality of a certain student's writing. I was reflecting on the fact that this student always does a good job, no matter what the assignment. As I sort through a plethora of papers daily, many of which sound alike or meet minimum requirements, it is always refreshing when I get to hers, truly a treat and not a chore. This is a blessing to me. I was compelled to write her a note and attach it to her graded paper.

I keep a variety of notecards in my desk at school for just this purpose. Some of these are "thank you" cards; some have inspiring words such as "Believe" or "Wish" or "Success" on them; others have quotes from literature, such as "Sometimes I've believed as many as six impossible things before breakfast." (Lewis Carroll) I have learned just how much it means to my students to receive a personal, handwritten note wishing them success on a sports outing, or appreciating that they went the extra mile on an assignment. So often we think about or notice positive things in others but don't share them. We ought to. It might be just what that person needs on that day. It only takes a little effort to make a big difference. Tell those students you appreciate them!

November 21, 2013

I am thankful that I have all these essays to grade over Thanksgiving break, because through them I see such amazing growth in my students, not only as writers and scholars but as people, too. Through these essays I see that what I am doing matters. I am thankful that my students all look and act so different. It reminds me that diversity is beautiful. It makes me flexible. I am thankful that they cannot be trusted to do everything right, such as go to the bathroom when they say that is where they are going. This keeps me on my toes. I am thankful they ask me questions I can't answer because it means they are thinking for themselves. I am thankful when I have to reteach so that I may find a better way.

I am thankful for my students because they make me laugh. They give me a reason. They make me a better person than I would be without them. So, I am thankful for these dang essays. That's my story and I am sticking to it.

SOURCES

Beers, Kylene and Probst, Robert E. (2011) "Literature as a 21st-Century Skill." *Language Arts Journal of Michigan*: Vol. 26: Issue. 2. Article 4. http://dx.doi.org/10.9707/2168-149X.1792

Boyles, Nancy. "Closing in on Close Reading." Educational Leadership. Vol. 70.4. December 2012/January 2013. 36-41.

Brookhart, Susan. "Starting the Conversation About Grading." Educational Leadership. Vol. 69.3. Nov. 2011.

Broz, William J. "Not Reading: The 800 Pound Mockingbird in the Classroom" English Journal. 100:5. 2011: 15-20.

Cain, Sean and Mike Laird. *The Fundamental 5: The Formula For Quality Instruction*. 2011 Sean Cain and Mike Laird.

Callaghan, Patsy. "Literature and Ecology: Integrating Story, Science, and Standards." English Leadership Quarterly. April 2013:3.

Griggs, Cynthia A., Barbara H. Davis, and Marisa Garcia. *English in Texas*. Vol 42.1. Spring/Summer 2012.

Guskey, Thomas. "Five Obstacles to Grading Reform." Educational Leadership. Vol 69.3. Nov. 2011.

Jago, Carol. "Opening the Literature Window." Educational Leadership. ASCD:40. March 2012.

Livingston, Michael. "The Infamy of Grading Rubrics." English Journal. 102.2 (Nov 2012): 108-113.

LoMonico, Michael. "These words are not mine": Are We Still Teaching Literature When We Use Adaptations?" English Journal. Vol. 102:2. Nov. 2012: 14.

Maxwell, John. *The Fifteen Invaluable Laws of Growth*. New York: John C. Maxwell, 2012.

Page, Melissa. "Popular Culture: The New Literacy Challenge for English Teachers." English Journal. 102:2 Nov. 2012: 129-133.

Paul, Anne Murphy. "Your Brain on Fiction." New York Times Sunday Review. March, 2012.

Pilgrim, Jodi and Christie Bledsoe. "An Investigation of Technology in the Classroom and Its Impact on Literacy Education." English in Texas. Vol. 42:2. Fall/Winter 2012.

Prensky, Marc. "Our Brains Extended." Educational Leadership. March, 2013. ASCD.

Rapp, Katie. "Quality Feedback." Educational Leadership. Vol. 54:7. July, 2012.

Rothman, Robert. "A Common Core of Readiness." Educational Leadership. Vol 67:7. April, 2012:14.

Strickland, James. "Writer's World 2.0: The Times They Are A'changin'" English Leadership Quarterly: August, 2009.

Tomlinson, Carol Ann and Edwin Lou Javius, "Teach Up for Excellence" Educational Leadership. Vol. 69:5, Feb. 2012.

Wormeli, Rick. "Redos and Retakes Done Right." Educational Leadership. Vol 69:3. Nov. 2011

NOTES AND REFLECTION

"Though I lack the art to decipher it, no doubt the next chapter in my book of transformations is already written. I am not done with my changes."

—Stanley Kubrick

Notes and Reflection